TRIFECTA

- BOOK ONE -
R. CHARLES CARR

ANAID PUBLISHING

TRIFECTA

- BOOK ONE -

R. CHARLES CARR

This book is a work of fiction. Names, places, events, businesses, organizations and incidents contained within this work are either the product of the author's own imagination or are used fictitiously. The fashions in which they are presented are used for dramatic effect; they are not meant as a presentation or representation of the author's own beliefs.

Any resemblance to actual persons, living or dead, or actual events is entirely coincidental.

Published by ANAID PUBLISHING
ISBN: 978-0-9827997-0-3

ANAID PUBLISHING
P.O. Box 37161 Maple Heights, Ohio 44137
Email:Publisher@TrifectaTheBook.com

Cover Art: "Temptation" by Carly Short
Copyright © Carly Short - Used by Permission

www.TrifectaTheBook.com

Preface:

What you have before you is the first in three books of three separate stories which together make up their own sort of Trifecta. All three novellas are continued throughout the subsequent Trifecta books in serialized fashion until the day each of their specific stories are completed and the voices that speaks for each speak no more.

Though the Truth is in some of the fiction you have before you; some on its surface, some contemplatively hidden; from the time you open it's pages, until its set aside and shelved, it still as a whole remains a work of fiction never created to purport a particular point of view or agenda.

Regarding *"The Dream Pastor"*

As a Christian, I struggled with Intimidation's initial harsh and quite honestly vulgar language. Though a few 'unsavory' words still remain, much of it has been edited out of the final draft. This type of language appears only briefly and for the most part is non-existent through out the rest of the Trifecta. The explicit details which at one point graphically illustrated Michael's dreams have also been removed. It is due to my own spiritual growth over time that has led me to edit out the amount of carnality that existed within the first drafts of "The Dream Pastor". I would like to think that not only has the story remained faithfully intact, but also my current witness as a Christian.

Regarding *"Six-One-Twelve"*

Six-One-Twelve was originally a screenplay created as a pilot for a proposed television series. Several times I have attempted to convert it into story book form for its inclusion in the Trifecta; each time it came off as forced and quite simply just never seemed to work for me. I remain captive to the type of pacing and visualization the screenplay format affords this particular story which led to the decision in leaving at least its presence in Book One in the format it was written.

Screenplays are incredibly easy to read, a format most will quickly catch on to and I believe enjoy. Still, I have included before its title page a handful of definitions for reference of a few commonly used terms which might not be readily understood out of context to the uninitiated. It is my hope the format resonates well with you the reader and pulls you quickly into the story and battle.

*Regarding "**The Third Adam**"*

It will be obvious to the reader that the philosophy of metaphysics was definitely standing in the shadow of a corner in the room where this story was written. As the story continues to unfold in the subsequent Trifecta books themes such as eschatology and others are introduced and become even more prevalent. Out of the three stories within Book One, '*The Third Adam*' more so than the other two would best be described as science fiction and because of its depth within that genre requires the most investment from the reader. I hope you find its story both original and unique. It demanded its own special place in my head and a certain stillness of mind to pen.

R. CHARLES CARR

For Tai,

Dreams That Begin
Within One Construct
Can Come To Fruition
Within Another.

TRIFECTA: Book One

THE
DREAM
PASTOR

Tracy never stopped typing as she looked up at him. The longing her eyes imparted matched the desire that had been aching in him for quite some time…

Michael opened his eyes slowly, it was as if the dream he was having had a life and will of its own, not allowing him to wake until it was done with him. His bedroom was completely dark; that's the way he liked it, devoid of any sight or sound. If he had his way, he would sleep in a sensory deprivation tank, anywhere which would assist in allowing his nights to become concentric to the noise and chaos that usually was his day.

He became troubled as the guilt began to bear its weight down on him while he lay in the dark contemplating the sexual nature of his dream. In a couple of days, he would no-longer be Minster Michael Parks, but Pastor. It bothered him that on the eve of taking such a big step in his faith another dream might indeed be suggesting he had a deeper issue which lay dormant deep within him.

In the dark there was no where for him to fixate his stare. It wouldn't have mattered, light or dark his gaze was locked on to the memories of several of his most recent dreams, all sexual in nature, all with a twist. Each night the woman was different, either someone he knew in his wakened state, or a complete stranger; but it was the twist that disturbed him the most. Last night it was Tracy, a co-worker who periodically pre-occupied his thoughts; thoughts which easily would turn into fantasy if he didn't check them. Last nights dream stayed true to the common denominator that was prevalent in most of the dreams, that being they occurred in places which were both real and familiar, never becoming changed or distorted by the dreamscape but the twist, the people in his dreams literally in some way shape or form would be different; perhaps their complexion would be changed, as in pale or a natural soft speaking voice turned deep within the dreaming.

'Where in his psyche was all this coming from?' he wondered.

A couple of nights ago while dreaming, he met a beautiful woman who rang his doorbell. She realized she had the wrong address but still asked if she could come in; one thing quickly led to another as she wasted no time in shedding her clothes. The twist… the long tail which came out her backside, its length stopping short of touching the floor.

As Michael continued to ponder in the darkness… he fell back asleep.

An old albino stood in the distance at one end of the alley… watching. His frame bent at the shoulders, hunched over a cane for support. His skin cracked and fractured, like a desert terrain long dried from exposure. Gray patches of un-kept matted hair appeared in various spots on his head; there where sections of scalp which hung tenuously from loose pieces of skin. None of the dirty tattered clothes he wore matched. Though it was daytime, the brightness of the sun didn't necessitate the small round sun glasses he wore to cover his eyes. The old albino slowly waved, gesturing Michael toward him. A certain fear gripped Michael as the old man's mouth spread to a smile, that's when Michael felt a hand on his shoulder causing him to jump so that he was again awake.

—— —— ——

The images in Michael's dreams disturbed him so that at one point he considered not accepting the pastoral position which was being offered to him. One thing he knew for sure; while awake God was definitely using him to positively affect the lives of others, despite his strange dream time experiences. At some point he began to consider maybe the source of his dreams were perhaps satanic; maybe the enemy was trying to sideline his future service to God and his ministry by causing him to question his own spiritual integrity?

'Is a man accountable for his actions while dreaming?"

The Baptist church where Michael served as a minister was one of the more prominent churches in Southern Georgia with a congregation close to seven hundred and growing. Even though he worked full time as the assistant to the Chief Financial Officer of a large bearing manufacturing company; the last year and a half he still managed to free up enough of his personal time to perform his ministerial duties which were delegated to him by Pastor Ryan, the founder of New Hope Missionary Baptist Church. Pastor Ryan told

Michael ultimately the church would like to hire him on full time as an Associate Pastor; but the church needed to continue to grow both in membership and finances before adding more to it's current staff. For now, everyone else in the ministry worked on a volunteer basis, fitting their ministerial duties in between their time at work and what they were spending with their families.

Michael finally pushed himself out of bed. He promptly made his way into the bathroom where he stood for more than a moment staring into the mirror.

'*How well did he really know himself?*' he wondered.

He finally picked up his toothbrush and paste; the rhythm of the brushing helped to keep his thoughts moving forward.

'*Sometimes the best way to address a potential problem is simply just expose it.*'

Later today, he decided he'd give Jason a call. Jason was a fellow minister at New Hope and a close friend, something of which he didn't have in quantity. Both Michael and Jason had shared quite a bit of their past with one another, something of which at times was painful to do. They both knew with confidence that whatever they shared would always stay between the two of them.

—— —— ——

As usual Michael got to work early, he knew if he hung out much longer in the break room he either would run into Tracy when she came down to put her lunch in the employee refrigerator or Ethel who got her first fill of coffee before heading to her office. Both Tracy and Ethel were members of New Hope. Michael knew Ethel had a crush on him which at times she was not ashamed to show. On the other hand, Tracy was sort of an enigma; when it came to Michael discerning if she had any real feelings toward him or not; she always reverted to calling him 'sir' if the conversation got a little too 'familiar'.

Ethel was the first out of the two women to show up...

"Morn'n Michael" she greeted, becoming all teeth and giggle as he replied.

Ethel was the supervisor of their company's administrative support staff. She sang in the churches choir while also volunteering her time as an administrative assistant to Pastor Ryan.

She had a pretty face, accentuated by uncommonly light brown eyes and a smile that could light up any room in which it was introduced. She was also a good deal over weight, an aspect of Ethel which didn't negate the special type of attention her natural attractiveness typically garnered. Michael liked her well enough; though not in the same vain which could lead him to reciprocate the feelings she had for him; without a doubt, he knew one day she would make someone a great wife.

"Do you think I'll be able to sneak a couple of items in the budget I sent you yesterday" she asked trying to make conversation.

"No changes after final submission, you know the rules" he answered in a false matter of fact fashion.

Ethel fended a fake pout, while still managing to smile with her eyes.

"Well," he started, "since you put it that way, and considering it's still in my inbox..."

It was a favor he had no problem in extending. Michael like several others had caught wind Ethel was going through some personal issues, though he didn't know the specifics. Maybe it would explain why she's had to take so much personal time off as of late.

The smile on her face returned, bigger than before as she placed a hand on his arm.

"Thanks, I really appreciate that."

Then with as much mocked professionalism as possible she further offered...

"If there's anything I can do to return the favor... just let me know."

The faint glint in her eye suggested the *anything* might be willing to lend itself to being something that could exist outside of the scope of what one employee would normally reciprocate towards another.

"Thanks" he said, "I'll keep that in mind."

Michael surprised himself in the manner in which he delivered his reply. Definitely a bit open ended considering their statue as two people of the faith. By the book he knew it wasn't proper...

'After all' he told himself. *'It not like it could possibly lead to anything.'*

The delivery of his reply had him once again questioning whether or not he should be stepping into the position which was being offered to him. Truth be told, with the dreams he's been having, he was starting to question whether if he should still be ministering.

Both his thoughts and conversation with Ethel were interrupted by Tracy walking into the room. The office attire she wore was always both appropriate and professional, though she'd literally have to wear a burlap bag to hide her curvaceous figure. Tracy's nails always stood out to him, nicely manicured and painted; accented by a small graphic design glued to each. Being a detail freak, he always was attracted to those who took the time to pay attention to the little things that accented the whole. Her red shoes perfectly matched the color of her lipstick. For the last week of so, she wore her naturally curly hair straight, its length passing just slightly beyond her shoulders.

Though Michael and Ethel's conversation remained innocent enough, he couldn't help but feel somewhat uneasy in Tracy's presence. Tracy unlike Ethel did not participate in any ministry or church activity, yet she was always faithful with her attendance and tithe.

Tracy greeted the both of them before going into a conversation about the most recent broadcast of "American Idol". It was a conversation Michael couldn't take part in; he didn't watch much television. He filled his coffee mug one last time, biding them both an adieu as he left the room.

When he got to his desk he logged into his computer and immediately accessed his email. He sent a message to his friend Jason asking if it were possible they could meet for dinner at Applebee's. Jason immediately replied with his confirmation. Michael then sent an email to Ethel informing her of the amount of time she had to modify her budget before he was forced to forward what he had to his boss, their employer's CFO.

"You've got two hours sister", he typed ending the words with a colon followed by a closed parenthesis forming the all too familiar 'smiley face'.

Michael was now ready to pour himself into the pile of spreadsheets, voice and emails that awaited.

Several Hours Later...

Accounting was on the second floor at the end of a hall that contained six offices, one of which being Michael's. He looked up and out of the large picture window that allowed him to see into the hall and spotted Tracy who evidently was coming towards his office, but suddenly turned and walked away.

"Now what was that was all about?" he wondered.

Michael pushed it as far as it would go to the back of his mind, moved his mouse to interrupt the screen saver on his desktop and continued to work.

Dinner...

Michael ended the call on his cell phone, flipping it closed as he dropped it on the passenger seat. He was talking to Jason who informed him he was already inside the restaurant at their table. Michael parked the car, walked inside and made his way over to where Jason was sitting.

"Hey, Brother" Jason stood greeting him with a hug, his voice both deep and relaxed.

Jason wore a polo shirt which was doing very little to conceal the fact he was about fifty pounds over weight, though it was spread well over his six foot two frame, there was still that ever present gut which made itself known as it hung out a bit over his belt. The temples of his hair were graying, though his face still maintained a youthful appearance considering he was approaching the age of forty-one.

They briefly went over the usual consequential stuff that made up their day; then hit upon some church related topics here and there before getting to the real reason why Michael wanted to meet with him. It was Jason who switched the topic of conversation in the direction that Michael needed it to go.

"Evidently, something is definitely bothering you Brother" Jason observed. Michael waited to reply until the waitress was done with her business of taking their orders and removing the dinner menus. Jason picked up his glass, took a long sip of coke and went right to it...

"For about a month or so, I have been having these weird, disturbing sometimes even sexual dreams; at times they are women I know, others not".

Michael paused to allow Jason to react. He knew it was going to be one or the other, either the 'don't worry about, it's just the enemy trying to get at you' reaction or 'this is serious, and you need to pray and seek the Lord'.

Jason looked slightly away, as if he were in conference with someone inside his own head, he was patient as he allowed his spiritual discernment to weigh in, a discernment he taped into as he asked his question...

"Besides the sex, what are some of the other details... any odd stuff?"

Michael was starting to feel uncomfortable, as he began to detail the more obscure aspects of his dreams.

Jason, definitely one of the Lord's faithful was also one of the most objective people Michael knew; despite being close friends, Michael knew it was both Jason's wise counsel and objectivity that he could count on. When he was done, Michael leaned back and emptied what was left in his glass. The waitress returned with their dinners, Michael was surprised to find he had talked so long that enough time had expired for both of their meals to be prepared.

Jason waited as the waitress placed everything before them. She caught the subtle hint and picked up her pace and left.

Jason knew it took quite a bit for Michael to divulge what he told him, despite their friendship and especially on the eve of Michael's pastoral appointment. Jason looked down at his food as he ate, contemplating how to unpack the Socratic style of questioning which he was so fond.

"So, what do you think? What are you options?"

Michael knew the true nature of the question and faced it head on with his answer...

"I'm really thinking about turning away from the Pastorate Brother".

Most ministers Jason knew became so for a myriad of reasons, they had a gift to preach, perhaps they had a strong need to serve their fellow man within the Christian framework, or they in fact had a pastoral gift that was latent within them. It was these types of gifts that drove them to the ministry. Jason knew Michael well enough to know he definitely had many of those gifts; but what Jason never had come forward to tell Michael was that for a while now he didn't feel Michael was ready to take on becoming a

Pastor. He never brought it up only because he couldn't pinpoint the exact reason for his doubt. Hearing what was being told to him now only confirmed his belief regarding that 'something', and that all along it must have been his spiritual discernment trying to break through the layers of friendship that was between them.

Jason sat for a minute, hoping Michael would ask the one question which would open the door allowing him to speak with as much honesty and as uninhibited as he desired, as was needed. Jason knew he would have no choice and it would be his duty as a friend and even more so, as a minister of God to give Michael his full opinion as to what his next steps should be.

'Thank God' Jason thought, as Michael finally got to that question...

"What would you do if you were me?"

Jason allowed a slight pause so Michael wouldn't think he had actually arrived at an opinion before the question was posed. which of course he did.

"In all honestly Brother, if I were you... I wouldn't take the position, evidently there's an issue of the flesh that's deep, that still needs to be worked out; of course mixed in there with the gifts God has given you, but never the less it is there."

Michael was not surprised at what he was hearing, it really was something he knew all along, it just sat better with him hearing it come from someone other than himself; someone he trusted who loved the church and Jesus at least as much as he did.

"So, I should step down as a Minister too; maybe have a talk with Pastor Ryan?" Michael asked.

"I don't think you need to go that far, but there just might indeed be some territory you and he should cover."

Michael chewed both on the steak in his mouth and their conversation. Though Jason was providing some serious wise council, it was time to stop avoiding the inevitable and to set up that meeting with Pastor Ryan.

A television hanging from the ceiling in the near distance was showing an old episode of 'Seinfeld', Jason used it to change the subject. Both men continued to eat, laughing together as they departed from the conversation that initially brought them together for the evening.

— — —

Michael set the alarm clock to turn on at six thirty a.m.. Though he was naturally an early riser, he thought he'd play it safe anyway. He then crawled in bed; it had been an exhaustive day, he definitely was ready to go to sleep, though not looking forward to any type of dreaming whatsoever.

He was now drifting in and out, eyes closed as he played back bits and pieces of the conversation he had earlier with Jason. He repeated over again the same thoughts and contemplations he played in his mind while driving home. He decided at the earliest opportunity he was going to schedule a meeting with Pastor Ryan and as gracefully as possible decline the offer that was being placed before him. The verdict was still out as to whether or not he would tell him more than the perfunctory 'I'm not ready, I just need a little bit more time for God to deal with me '. He knew full well the possibility that Pastor Ryan might push further to know the real reason why he was declining the opportunity, but considering there was nothing he did wrong... at least in an awakened state, he didn't feel there was necessarily a need for full disclosure, at least not yet. He knew part of his decision to keep all the facts from Pastor Ryan was because he feared he might ask him to step down from his ministerial duties as well. It was selfish to be driven and think along those lines, but Michael enjoyed serving as a minister, he enjoyed serving the Lord.

What Michael didn't know was if he had not so erroneously let the voice of that belief become so loud and strong, he would have heard his own spiritual discernment telling him to not only divulge all to Pastor Ryan, but that his dreams truly where demonic attacks, and because of some of the choices he made within them that maybe stepping away from the ministry wasn't such a bad idea. It was a voice that his flesh and his own desires squelched; a voice if heard should have perhaps been listened to, whose message he needed to yield.

—— —— ——

Michael was at the very edge of entering a dream, each time he nodded off, his body involuntarily would shake him out of it; a ritual he seemed to follow every night before taking that final plunge into sleep. This night, something else took him from the last moments from wake to dream. It was a faint noise, but clearly it was the sound of a television. Michael lived in a ranch style home, every room was on the same level, and though the square footage was spacious, not so much so that he couldn't hear the crash of something breaking on the hardwood floor far off in the living room.

He definitely was now fully awake, startled and scared. He reached over to pick up the cordless phone that was sitting on the night stand next to the lamp he used for reading. He quickly dialed 911, each ring a strong pounding in his heart until it was answered.

"911 what's you're emergency?"

Trying to remain calm, he quickly gave the operator the information she requested, then listened as she gave him instructions as what to do.

"Sir, whatever you do, don't go in to the area of the house where you believe the intruder to be; if you can climb out of a window, hide under the bed or go in to a closet that is what you need to do; and whatever you do, don't hang up the phone. Help is on the way."

Michael started to make his way towards the bedroom window when he remembered that it sticks really badly when you try to open it, it also made quite a bit of noise when slid upwards. He tried to make his way towards the closet, that's when he heard someone calling him from the living room.

"Come on out here Michael!"

The voice was strong, loud and old. It startled him so that he dropped the phone he was holding. It hit the floor hard, causing the back cover to pop off. The yellow square battery inside came out, dangling by the small red and back wires which kept it attached to the phone. The call was disconnected. A raspy, cough and phlegm filled laughter erupted from the living room; then the voice spoke in a demanding tone that strengthened the paralysis that took hold of Michael.

"Boy, get your narrow ass in here! If I have to get up and come get you, it won't be pretty!"

Michael managed to will his feet to move in the direction towards his living room. It took all he had to force the seized muscles in his legs to cooperate. Before he left the bedroom, he picked up the only thing he saw which possibly could be used for a weapon, a wire hanger which hung on a hook on the inside of his bedroom door. He realized his hands were shaking as he made his way down the hall.

He peaked his head slowly in the living room, all the lights where off except for the lamp on the table that was directly to the right of the couch. There was another table on its left, but the lamp that normally was on it had broken into several large pieces when it hit the hardwood floor. Michael jumped back, shocked by the sight of seeing the old albino from his dreams sitting on his couch.

"Sorry to wake you brother, sorry about the lamp too... I guess I'm just not as graceful as I use to be. I must admit, I'm a bit more comfortable walking around in darkness, my eyes don't like the light."

The old man erupted in laughter showing an array of broken and missing teeth. It looked as if someone took a baseball bat to his mouth.

"Well boy sit down, sit down... after all it's your house ain't it?"

Michael complied, slowly taking a seat in the chair on the opposite side of the coffee table now separating him and the old man. *'Where were the cops?'* he wondered.

Michael looked at the hanger in his hand; he couldn't find the strength to open it, to let it go.

"How did you get in here? What do you want?" Michael asked.

"First things, first... I know you've been seeing me around, we've been long over due for a formal introduction... my name is rather long; truth be told, it's been quite a spell since I've had to pronounce it. I'd probably get it wrong anyway... you can call me by my nickname, I've been using it so long most think it's my real one anyway, they call me Intimidation, 'Tim' for short."

Intimidation sat there smiling, beaming from the fact he knew his name was well earned. Michael started to speak, but Intimidation cut him short.

"Look, I know you got a lot of questions, but the fact is my time is short, and I have to move on, so here it is son plain and simple. You recently had an important decision to make and it appears you made the right choice. You my friend becoming 'Pastor Michael' would have been... well lets just say problematic for all concerned. Being the way 'second thoughts' work and all... I thought I'd come by and encourage you to stay with that choice and never ever change your mind."

Michael wanted to sit back into the chair, but he couldn't force the muscles in his back to relax.

"If I do?" he asked.

Intimidation's demeanor froze as he wiped his aged, leathery forehead with the back of one of his hands...

"Well friend..." He removed the dark glasses which hung on his face, exposing two cataract laden eyes...

"I'd have no choice but to let those who really want to bust you up do so."

Intimidations stare pierced him deep. There was no denying the sincerity as to what he was telling him.

"But why?" Michael asked.

Michael's mind couldn't wrap around the fact his ministry could have a serious impact outside his own personal context, irrespective to whatever choice he made.

"Let's just say we don't need your destiny dancing with nor stepping on the toes of ours". Intimidation replied.

Intimidation slowly rose with some effort, speaking as he walked over to the television, cutting it off...

"Wasn't shit on anyway, shame... I don't get out often".

Intimidation opened the door to let himself out; he looked back at Michael who sat still staring at him in both confusion and fear. "Help is on the way!" Intimidation shouted sarcastically back at him in the same voice and manner as the 911 operator. Even after the door closed, he could still clearly hear Old Tim's taunt.

"See ya' on the flip side son!"

—— —— ——

Michael woke to find he had fallen asleep on the couch in the living room.

He looked down towards his feet and discovered he must have kicked over the lamp which sat on the end table at the other end of the couch. It lay in pieces on the floor. He was still groggy from a sleep which delivered no rest as he made his way down the hall to his bedroom to get dressed. He turned the alarm clock off before it had the chance to reach its set time, which was only three minutes from now. As he walked to his dresser he suddenly froze, on the floor laid his cordless phone broken open in the same fashion he remembered from what he erroneously believed was a dream.

Michael made it into work early as usual, but too mentally wound up to take his regular stroll down to the break room. He didn't know what to make of what transpired in his home last night. He knew it definitely wasn't a dream. The encounter happened, and he was certain the sooner he got his mind to embrace that fact the better off he'd might be.

For quite awhile now he had been a minister of the Lord; during this time he had met people who claimed to have had supernatural visitations, and in some cases even attacks; but since he never personally experienced anything like it for himself, he could only believe in their occurrences from a distance, accepting in several cases what they said to be true only because supernatural encounters and attacks did exist within the belief framework of his Christian faith. If he were to deny their existence, he would have to deny a vital part of that framework, thus putting into question his Christian faith as a whole. Admittedly, he had never heard of anything remotely close to the visit he received.

It's a fact that most policemen in their whole career never get the opportunity to fire their gun in the line of duty, and when that opportunity does happen it's typically not for a good reason. Along the same lines, it can be said for ministers serving in the Body of Christ... even far less the number of them would ever get the chance to face a supernatural manifestation of the likes of his encounter with Intimidation.

There was no going back now. The irony being before Intimidation's visit Michael's mind was made up to back away from not only the pastorate, but ministry all together. Now he wasn't so sure; it appears Tim's little visit may have had the opposite effect on him...

Until now certain aspects of his faith where just that... faith, faith in believing a conflict waged between mankind and the powers of this dark world and against the supernatural forces of evil in the heavenly realms. If anything, Intimidations visit did nothing but confirm and solidify Michael's belief in God, His Word and the purpose that Christ placed within him, no matter how buried in the flesh some of his issues may be. Now that evil demonic forces were a tangible actuality which he had personally experienced, then so too must be the Lord's providence as it relates to Man. Michael was sure now was not the time to back away from the conflict no matter the risk or consequence, but to allow himself to be used by the Light to draw out and combat the enemy.

— — —

Locked in much thought and reverie, he didn't notice Tracy was standing in his office doorway.

"Excuse me, is this a bad time?" Tracy's eyes gave way to something which appeared to seriously be troubling her.

"No, not at all", he answered..."Grab a seat" he motioned with his hand at one of the two chairs in front of his desk. She looked down the hall as she slowly shut the door behind her and entered.

"I feel a little weird coming to you; especially here at work, but...well I just need someone to talk to and someone who can keep my business to themselves; since you being a minister and all at the church, it just kind of made sense to come to you."

Michael tried to put on his best game face, something he usually did when he spoke to Tracy so she wouldn't perceive his attraction towards her.

"Don't worry about it..."he started. "I'm who I am both in and out of work, so where do we begin?"

"I'm a little embarrassed to say, but I have this problem... I've been seeing a guy for about seven months his name is David, things are pretty bad between us."

Michael looking at her... "You're always by yourself at church?"

Tracy's reacted with a short laugh... "He's not the type of guy you'd see at church."

"So how did you hook up with him?" He asked.

"I met him in a supermarket parking lot, my shopping cart got away from me and it ran into his car. He told me he'd forget all about the big scratch it made if I met him once for dinner. He was a little charming and pleasant at the time so I did. After that, we just kept seeing each other. In the beginning it was sort of nice, but after a while he started talking to me differently, like he owned me. He expects me to tell him everywhere I've been and where I am going. That stuff starts to get old after a while so I told him I needed a break."

"What was his reaction?" Michael asked.

Tracy got up, walked to Michael's door then opened it to see if anyone was coming down the hall. She shut it as she began to walk towards him as she spoke...

"First he pushed me down, then he kicked me". Tracy stopped and lifted her blouse to expose the large black and blue bruise which spread across her mid section..."I was going to talk to you the other day, but chickened out at the last minute." Michael's eyes widened in both disgust and disbelief.

"Did you call the police?" he asked

"I was going to, but he begged me not too, that's when I found out he's on probation. I told him not to call or speak to me again."

"So how long did that last?" Michael asked.

"Only for about a day or two" she responded. "He called me this morning before I came to work."

"You know it's not too late to call the police" Michael offered.

Tracy got up and turned her back to him, not able to look him in the face as she continued...

"Well I wanted him to leave, but I guess I also wanted to tick him off a little too... I told him I hooked up with one of my old boyfriends and that me and my 'ex' were going to try to kick it again... I think I just made things worse".

"So who is this old boyfriend, if you don't mind me asking?" Michael pressed.

She turned to Michael throwing up both hands in exasperation..."There is no old boyfriend".

"Well this is a no brainer, you need to go to the police and tell them everything, then show them that bruise."

He could tell the advice he was giving her was not sinking in; slightly frustrated he changed his approach.

"I tell you what, play hard ball with him one last time, and if that doesn't work you definitely should go to the police before this gets any uglier; tell him that's what you are going to do if he calls or comes near you again. Take pictures of the bruise and let him know you have them, but you need to be firm, and you need to do it... if he ever calls you after that again."

When Michael was done, Tracy at first stared at him blankly; it was hard to read her, to tell whether or not the advice made its impression. A nervous smile slowly grew across her face as she made her next request...

"Can I have your phone number?"

Michael sat back in his seat trying not to look too surprised or even worst... pleased.

"It's just... I'm going to take your advice, and well, if you don't mind I might need someone to talk to afterwards that's all."

It was all quite clear; all the bells and whistles were going off telling him it was about now where he should be drawing that line in the sand; to back away and assist Tracy in hooking up with one of the female ministers at the church. He was well aware that his attraction to her was preventing him from doing so; needless to say, he found himself giving her the number.

"Thank you, I won't bug you, but I'm glad I have it... just in case" she offered.

A small awkward moment passed between them, then she headed toward the door to leave, she stopped as she remembered one more thing she wanted to ask...

"How well do you really know Ethel?"

The question caught Michael by surprise.

"What do mean, like are we seeing each other or something?" Tracy's demeanor didn't change, though she realized she might be starting a conversation she wasn't equipped to finish.

"No, not at all it just... never mind".

The question troubled Michael on another level. Ethel as of late had been taking a lot of time off from work. She never did reply to his email or sent the modified budget to him. What if something is seriously wrong with her?

"Is there something I should know Tracy" he asked pointedly.

"No... just wondering, thanks again" she replied as she hurriedly disappeared into the hallway.

— — —

It was well into the night two days later when Michael received Tracy's call. It wasn't hard to tell she was upset.

"I'm sorry to bother you so late. I talked to David the other day, and told him one last time just like you and I talked about, but he just called. I'm going to call the police in the morning, but I don't want to be alone, and I've got no place to go. Is it possible you can come over?"

Michael knew the right answer was no, besides...

'How hard could it be for her to go someplace else, like a hotel? It's not like the police aren't open twenty – four seven.'

Despite knowing better he agreed.

He was familiar with the location. She rented a townhouse in a development on the southeast side of town. While he drove, he repeatedly told himself that at the first hint of he finding himself or her starting to 'operate' out of bounds that he would immediately leave; he continued to beat into his own head he was only going over there to '*minister*' to her and just be a '*friend*'.

The door opened though she was wearing a robe, he could see part of the blouse and blue jean pants she had on underneath, '*well thank God she has clothes on*' he thought. As she let him in, he could tell she had been crying. They sat and talked awhile, mostly about church and work, it wasn't long before they noticed the sound of a car pulling in to the driveway. Tracy made her way to the window, pulling the curtain back just enough so she could see out.

"Oh my God, It's him!" she exclaimed as the sound of the car shut off.

Michael got up to take a look for himself. The notion came to him to do something, something that was against his better judgment.

"What are you doing?" she asked in a heated whisper and panic.

"I'm going out there" he stated flatly.

Michael open the front door, took two steps outside and stared in the direction of David's parked car. Physically, Michael wasn't imposing, yet he was far from small. David sat a moment longer in his car before simply turning it on, pulled out the driveway and drove away.

Tracy backed away from the window where she was standing both surprised and impressed. She never would have pictured David backing down from anyone. Tracy was still standing in the same spot when Michael returned...

"Thank you" she said softly.

"It figures…" Michael started. "Some guys play the bully when they don't think you'll stand up for yourself or no one has your back."

Tracy looked directly into Michael's eyes as she spoke

"Thanks for having my back."

"Thank God" Michael said attempting to break the moment up. "So now will you go to the police?"

"Yes, I promise. Can you help me? I want to get a picture of this bruise".

She reached into one of the robes pockets and pulled out a small digital camera and handed it to him. She then slid out of the robe and pulled up her shirt blouse just enough to expose the bruise he had seen a couple of days earlier. Some of the more severe coloration had disappeared, but the bruise as a whole was still quite present. She moved too fast for Michael to protest. He held up the camera and took a couple of pictures, managing to use its zoom for a closer view rather than bridging the distance physically. After a couple of clicks of the camera Tracy closed the space between them, placing her hand over his, looking into his eyes.

"You've been a great friend I'll probably be ok for the rest of the night. She backed away taking the camera out of his hand.

"I'm glad I could help...I guess" Michael slightly joked from his unease.

"You've gotta be sure to keep the ball rolling and do what you need to do with the police tomorrow. I'll see you in the morning." He offered attempting to get some control over the situation and his demeanor as he headed for the door. The look as if something was bothering her returned.

"I don't want to do this anymore" she said.

"Do what?"

"Pretend I don't have feelings for you, walk pass you and offer just a little wave and a smile, as if you don't matter no more than an empty chair behind a desk."

Michael was stunned. She looked at him waiting for him to say something. He slowly closed the door as she walked up to him, pressing against him staring into his eyes.

"Aren't you going to say something?" she asked.

"Well, there's a difference between what I feel versus what I should be saying. We both know what is right, which would be for me to leave."

He never got the chance to say anything more, she placed both of her hands gently on his face, kissing him deeply. He returned the kiss as the passion of her tongue entered his mouth. He picked her up, placing her on the couch.

"I have no business doing this..." he said as he unbuttoned her blouse.

"Then only make it half wrong" she offered." I want to be more than just 'tonight' to you... I wanted to be your woman."

The whole moment seemed surreal to Michael, something he thought about, but never would have imagined happening.

As she pulled him down on to her kissing him, she whispered in his ear that she would stay with him as long as he would have her. Afterwards, Minister Michael Parks and Tracy Scott had a very long night together.

The next day Michael arrived a little later than usual to work, though still before his scheduled start time. As he approached his office door he saw Tracy sitting in one of the chairs in front of his desk, she was using the tissue she held to wipe at the tears that were swelling in her eyes.

"What's wrong, David again?" he asked as he entered. She tried to smile but gave him a brief hug instead.

"No, something worst, its Ethel, she's dead."

Michael fell into the chair beside her in disbelief. As clergy, he was no stranger to death, but he didn't see this one coming, the news took his knees from under him.

"How?"

"She had a stroke. She told me months ago the problems her doctors were having trying to bring and keep her blood pressure down."

Just then Michael's phone rang bringing him out of his stupor. Tracy got up to leave so he could talk in private, but he motioned for her to stay. Several minutes went by before he placed the phone's headset back on its cradle. He looked up at her even more stunned then before.

"That was Ethel's sister, she and her family want me to do the funeral. They asked if I could stop by their house tonight."

"I'm not surprised Michael, she really liked you a lot."

"Yeah I know..." he replied. "I know."

—— —— ——

A little less than a week went by before the day of the funeral arrived. Michael cleared it with Pastor Ryan to be released to perform the ceremony, of which he had done an extraordinary job including a very thoughtful eulogy which the family really seemed to appreciate.

Every since that fateful night with Tracy, Michael had been able to sleep trouble free. Tracy and he continued to see each other, but agreed to limit the physical contact to hugs and infrequent kisses. Never-the-less, he had decided to step back from serving in ministry. He had informed Pastor Ryan of his intentions during the time he went to discuss his role in Ethel's funeral and of course the good Pastor wanted to know the real reason why he was stepping down, but Michael was able to get him to respect his desire to keep those reasons to himself, at least for awhile. Both men agreed Ethel's funeral would be Michael's last clergical duty. All seemed a bit better for a while until three days later, when Ethel returned to Michael in a dream.

—— —— ——

Michael was pushing a shopping cart down the isle at the local supermarket, that's when he saw her smiling, waving him over.

"Hey Minister!" she teased as she greeted him. Ethel looked stunning; instead of her large over weight body, she was now slim and curvy. She wore form fitting black paints and a matching black blouse which was connected to a white clergy collar that was about her neck. Her hair seemed to radiant a shine all its own. Ethel always had a special smile which now seemed to have the power to light up the heart as well. Michael was aware his eyes were filling with tears. He was definitely glad to see her, and deep in his very marrow knew it truly was Ethel who stood before him, not some apparition made up out of his nocturnal imagination or subconscious.

"That was one nice eulogy you gave" Ethel stated sincerely.

"Thanks" he offered…" I really miss seeing you at the office" he continued.

"God knows what he's doing besides…" she began while tugging on her clergy collar…"I got a new job now." She went to him, then lavished a huge hug.

"So how does this work? Shouldn't you be somewhere playing a harp" he asked half jokingly. None of this made sense., this was Ethel, someone who gave their life to Christ, why was she stuck in aisle six in a dream?"

"It doesn't always quite work like that" she offered. Being dead is sort of like attending a big church service. There are those who work to deliver the service, and those who get to sit and enjoy it. In death, those that serve allow the living to live, those in heaven to enjoy the after life and help send those to hell who should be there. I was chosen to serve the Kingdom in death, within the realm of the dreaming.

Michael scoffed at what he was hearing. It butchered a good portion of his belief system and personal theology. It wasn't hard for Ethel to discern the degree he was struggling with this, causing her to laugh. She gathered both of her arms around his right and led him out of the aisle.

"Never-the-less, when the living dream they travel either to one or two places the 'In' or the 'Out'. The 'In' is inside their own head and being, a place to allow the mind and spirit to go offline, refresh and entertain the will of the subconscious; then there's the 'Out' that's where we are now. Here in Purgatory Michael. This is where the Darkness snatches away the hopes and dreams of men, a place where he changes their destinies."

Ethel led him out of the supermarket into the open air. They walked across the street to a bench that was in front of a bus stop and sat. It was a bright and sunny day, a couple of children where riding their bikes along the sidewalk. A woman and child entered the supermarket they just left.

"The view is a lot different than some of your other dreams" She quizzed.

Michael instantly felt uncomfortable; somehow knowing she made reference to his explicit dreams from nights gone by. She pulled him closer to her to console his embarrassment.

"Don't feel that way, I'm not here to judge, but it is important you know there are few secrets here, someone or something is always watching.

It wouldn't be fair to judge you even if I could; the reasons why people make the decisions they do while dreaming are complicated, I think you'd admit there are things people do within them they'd never consider doing if they were awake, the meaning of accountability is somewhat shifted here in the Out".

He looked at Ethel, first asking though already knowing…

"But somehow something's different... the decisions I make here and now, they would be the same choices I'd make if I were awake wouldn't they?"

"You're catching on" she stated.

"At the moment you and I are sort of on the outside of the 'Out.'"

"So I'm not dreaming?" he asked.

"More close to what folk call lucid dreaming; though that wouldn't be entirely right since you're not exactly dreaming either."

"So let me get this straight, I'm in Purgatory, which actually turns out to be a dream, but I'm not dreaming?" Michael sarcastically quizzed.

Her voice became softer, a bit somber. "I'll have to explain that later". As she finished, a bus slowed towards their direction, pulling up to their stop.

"This is our ride" she said, leading him on to it. They both took a seat side by side about mid-way within its length.

"Where are we heading?" he asked sensing the direction and purpose within her."

"Hopefully where providence and your destiny will meet" she answered.

Ethel used their time riding to further explain the true nature of Purgatory. Michael was fascinated yet horrified as she went on to describe the dark beings that existed there and other facets of the realm.

Along with those that dreamed people who died sometimes ending up in Purgatory, though not to work out their sins or be punished before moving on. Some souls chose to stay to serve the Light, others to do the bidding of The Darkness. There were others who walked in Purgatory not because in death they were sent there, but purposely made their way there to visit loved ones while they slept within their dreams; others came to torment those who done them wrong before death.

Ethel shifted her explanation to the nature of Purgatory as a realm used by the Light and the Dark to war against one another and influence the hearts and minds of men.

She began describing demons who co-mingled within the dreams of the living, some who disguised themselves to fulfill the fantasies of those who slept, feeding their own lustful desires, and the more dangerous ones, demons that served the fallen angel Apollyon who used Purgatory to cause confusion within the subconscious of Man, confounding the call that is within all men to seek the Way, the Truth and The Light that will save their souls from eternal damnation.

Michael knew his bible well and was familiar with the reference to Satan's name in the Greek mentioned in Revelation 9:11. Apollyon is driven to destroy those whom God loves most Man; more specifically to corrupt man into destroying himself and each other. Apollyon used many fronts to wage his war, Purgatory was the perfect place to get inside the head and soul of Man while he slept, seeding his subconscious with thoughts and desires which would be buried there, waiting to manifest themselves at the right moment of temptation during the hours they were awake, a spiritual "Manchurian Candidate" by way of subtle demonic programming.

"So a man thinketh so is he" Ethel added as she quoted Proverbs 23:7, a bit of scripture that also applied to the subconscious.

The bus rode on, at each stop more people were getting off than on. In its front, two elderly women sat next to one another, they periodically conversing. One held a small paper shopping bag on her lap. In the back of the bus a much younger woman about her mid- twenties appeared to either have fallen asleep or become lost listening to whatever was being pumped into the earphones she wore.

The scenery on the outside drastically started to change, shadows were starting to fill complete spaces until the bus was now riding in total darkness save for the lights which radiated from its headlights. One of the old women pulled the cord above her head that ran along the upper wall of the bus, thus signaling to the driver a stop was desired. The bus slowed to a halt, but the doors remained closed. Both of the old women turned looking backwards towards the younger sleeping woman.

"What ever happens next..." Ethel warned.

"Don't interfere."

The old women got up and began to walk towards the back, one placed a wrinkled finger over her withered lips, smiling at Michael and Ethel, silently expressing her desire for them to remain both still and quiet. The woman walking carefully next to her reached into the bag she had and removed a small jar that contained a clear liquid. They continued towards the young sleeping woman.

The other old woman pulled out of her shirt pocket a small lighter. She tried to get it started; only a few sparks erupted as her thumb turned the small wheel against its flint.

The young woman was suddenly aware of them, her eyes staring in fear at the elderly women standing over her; she let out an unearthly screech which sounded like it came from an animal. Her mouth fell open exposing her toothless orifice. Instead of lips collapsing inward from lack of dental support, they curled backwards towards the outside of her face. She was a demon.

It jumped on to the woman who still was attempting to ignite the lighter, knocking it from her hand as it landed on her. They both crashed hard on to the floor of the bus. The other old woman flung the jar of fluid at the demons head. Glass erupted everywhere as the jar broke, its contents drenching the frantic demon and the old woman it had pinned to the floor. Michael fought the urge to bolt out of his seat to flee. The woman who threw the jar was now kicking at the head of the toothless demon. The blows did little to slow its crazed fervor as it continued to slam its fist into the head of the woman it sat on, the old woman underneath it worked to protect her face. It all would have seemed oddly comical if it weren't so horrific and brutal.

All the kicking finally managed to daze the demon who attempted to scamper away. The other elderly woman followed, her foot finding its mark as she continued striking downward.

The old woman still on the floor eyed the dropped lighter. It laid underneath one of the seats only an arms length away. She reached for it, turning the small wheel several times as the few sparks finally turned to flame.

"Step back Maggie!" she yelled as she engaged the small button locking the flame in, hurling the lighter at the screaming, battered demon.

The demon erupted in flames as the fluid covering it ignited, its legs flaying in the air as if it were drowning in a pool of watery fire whose surface it was trying to reach.

The bus driver swung out of his seat, but not before reaching for the fire extinguisher which hung to his left. He raced towards the back, pushing the two elderly women out of his way as he opened up its contents on the blackened, motionless body of the demon. A good portion of the back of the bus was now too in flames. Whatever was in the extinguisher was fast acting; the driver quickly had the fire extinguished. The smoke still present reached Ethel and Michael, they coughed profusely. The driver turned around, making his way back toward the front.

"Give me a second!" he said as he passed them. Out from the front they could hear him huffing and complaining.

"Sloppy, just plain sloppy!"

The driver hurriedly hit a couple of switches as he sat in his seat. Michael heard the sound of fans, the smoke dissipating. He realized it was being sucked to the outside; soon it and the fire were gone save for little thin wisps of smoke which floated lightly in the air and the lingering stench of burnt demon and bus. The driver opened the front and side doors. The two elderly women, faces now somewhat black from smoke made their way to the side door. Before exiting, one of them looked back at both Ethel and Michael.

"You both have a blessed day", she offered and was gone.

The driver closed the doors, and after two attempts the bus finally started. It slowly rolled forward as they continued along its route in the dark with Michael, Ethel and the burnt remains of a demon as passengers.

Michael looked at Ethel incredulously…

"Shouldn't we be getting off too?"

"It's not our stop." She replied.

After a bit of silence between them…

"What was that all about?"

"Purgatory couldn't exist if the Light or Dark could do just anything they wanted to against each other, there are rules; and there's a price to pay when they are broken" Ethel stated while gesturing towards the demon carcass behind them.

"Usually something that exists here can't destroy another unless the other broke a rule; Light and Dark are always looking, waiting for the other to break them so they can take advantage of the opportunity to lessen the others numbers, and trust me if you die here, you don't get to wake up… anywhere".

"You sure learned a lot for someone who only has been her for a little over a week." It was an observation Ethel was waiting for Michael to arrive; though now was not the time to break the news to him. She was curious how well he was going to handle it once he did. Michael was going to have enough to deal with when they got off the bus, it definitely was best to save the rest for later.

The bus slowed to a stop.

"I believe this is your stop Reverend" the driver announced, the rear and middle doors opening. Michael at first didn't bulge, not sure whether or not he wanted to brave the outside. They got off the bus stepping out on to what appeared to be a cul-de-sac. It was dimly lit by the light of one street lamp. Four houses faced them.

There was enough space for the bus to turn around. They both watched as it drove away into the night. Michael walked over to the street lamp as Ethel watched, promptly sitting down at its base.

"I'm not bulging until you explain what all this have to do with me?" he exclaimed.

"Shhh! Keep your voice down!" Ethel retorted as she hurried along side of him, pulling him up and over about thirty feet away from the light.

"We don't have time for this... look Michael you dedicated your life to Christ, the battle is even more intense on this side. You for whatever reason were chosen to lead and Pastor those of us who fight for Christ here so deal with it. The Darkness knows it and he won't be playing by the rules when he comes for you."

"Pastor" he replied sarcastically.

"Something like that" Ethel replied looking at him squarely so the seriousness of her reply wouldn't escape him.

"Ethel, you know yourself I'm not the best choice to Pastor anything... awake or sleep."

"It's because of those issues, the same issues the enemy wanted to use against you that make you the perfect choice... 'For in that He Himself has suffered being tempted, He is able to aid those who are tempted'" Ethel countered with Hebrews 2:18, scripture in which she knew Michael was familiar.

While Ethel continued he couldn't help but think of Tracy, and how unlike Jesus he yielded to some serious temptation both while dreaming and awake.

"The Light in this realm also need to be ministered to, along with the living that dream here to counter the influence of The Darkness; someone who can place a word of direction or encouragement into their subconscious so that perhaps one day, at the right time it will be enough of a whisper of influence to push them to walk in the right direction, to make the right choice."

A few moments paused before either of them said anything, Michael spoke first.

"You don't expect me to commit to anything now do you?"

Ethel folded her arms as she tried to stifle her frustration.

"You know Michael, sometimes certain decisions are taken right out of our hands and are simply made for us."

"What is that supposed to mean?" he asked.

"Later..." she answered "Right now we've got more important things to do."

"Such as?"

"The kind of business you saw on the bus; there's a demon in that house over there." Ethel stated pointing at the third house from the left.

"... a rather powerful one that's operating outside of any boundaries that confine most, he's come here tonight to kill someone living as they dream. It wants to kill a child Michael. I hope to God there's enough time left so we can do something about it".

Ethel told him the demon in question was none other than Intimidation. The first rule he broke was when he pushed himself to the other side of dreaming, the night he visited Michael in the flesh. Few demons had the strength or ability to cross over, but Intimidation was both very old and powerful. What exists in Purgatory is supposed to stay there. Intimidation was now going after a sleeping child, a child whose role within the 'Struggle' would one day be substantial. Demons were not allowed to plague the minds of children (though they periodically did so anyway), let alone kill them while they dreamt. The Darkness was getting desperate, and Ethel was sure there was a reason why. Fortunately because of his indiscretions, it was now open season on Intimidation, those of the Light were free to rip him apart.

"We're going up against a demon with our bear hands? At least those old ladies had a little fire and gasoline." Michael retorted.

They walked up to the house then entered it. Ethel picked up a toy aluminum bat that was lying on the floor. He tried to walk quietly, while doing so he inadvertently bumped in to a hall dresser, its top covered with several pictures within their frames fell loudly to the floor.

"The jig is up!!!" The old familiar voice howled with laughter from a room just at the top of the stairs.

Ethel and Michael took to the staircase jumping two to three steps at a time. At the top they rushed into the room where Intimidation had both of his hands around a small boy's neck, the child struggled while gasping for air. Michael dived on Intimidation, but the old man's body was as solid as a statue, he effortlessly bounced off of him. Intimidation threw the boy over the bed; he landed with a thud as his small body hit the floor on the other side. Intimidation leaped at Michael with incredible agility. Ethel tried to jump on him, but Intimidation violently back handed her in mid air. She went flying out of the room on to the floor like a rag doll hitting the top of the staircase, then tumbled downward, her body striking each and every step until she landed on the floor at its bottom. It was hard for her to move, pain erupting from joint and muscle as she tried. Intimidation was now on top of Michael, his old yet powerful hands about his neck.

Over and over again, Michael heard the words sounding off in his head 'You die in your sleep, you die forever' as he tried to pound his fist upwards at his assailants face, none of which was having any effect. Michael had no doubt that he was dying. Until recently he was certain what death would bring, the trust in his Christian faith had solidified that assurance, but now from all that he had learned, experienced and seen, much of that was now shaken.

'They that trust in the Lord ...' As those last words ran their course in Michael's head somewhere inside his being he heard the presence of a voice speak ...

"Trust in Me"

The words provided a strange comfort in the midst of his struggling, and for whatever reason Michael simply stopped resisting.

Suddenly there was a loud sound, similar to that of someone stepping their foot in to a watermelon, Intimidations mouth fell open as he shrieked in what Michael first thought was delight. Intimidations eyes rolled up into his head; through his wide open mouth Michael saw several small bloody fingers slowly moving, then they were gone as the blood in his mouth fell out over his bottom lip, some spilling on to his chest. Intimidation's body fell hard on the floor to the right of Michael. It lay there motionless except for an occasional spasmodic twitch, Intimidations unmoving eyes stared lifelessly at Michael.

Standing over Michael was the little boy, his left hand covered with blood from punching a hole through the back of Intimidations head. The child could not have been any older than seven or eight; he looked frightened.

"Are you ok?" Michael asked. The boy looked up for just a moment, eyes watery. He managed a faint smile and replied...

'They that trust in the Lord, shall be saved."

Ethel finally came out her daze from the impact of her head being banged about on the steps and worked her way back to the top of the stairs. She looked over at Intimidation's lifeless body then at the blood on the boy's hand.

"Tell me he didn't do that?" she asked sarcastically."

"Yes... and a good thing for me he did" Michael answered while rubbing his bruised neck. Ethel walked up to the boy, took his left hand, offered him a smile then led him out of the room.

Michael and Ethel took the boy down to the kitchen where the three of them sat at the small table, the boy drank a glass of water Ethel made for him.

"So when do I get to wake up?" asked Michael looking at Ethel, pushing his chair away from the table. Ethel couldn't look him in the eye; she sat there attempting to answer him as best she could.

"Michael I need to explain something to you." she began. He became agitated.

"You've done enough explaining already, I'm tired of this nightmare... now I'm ready to wake up and leave it!"

"Michael you're not going to wake up... you're dead."
He started to laugh, but the attempt didn't last long...

"You're kidding right?"

"Michael you died in your sleep from smoke inhalation as your house burned".

"When?" the question a whisper.

"Last night... sort of" she answered.

"What do you mean sort of?" he asked, anger mixing with disbelief.

"Well..."

Before she could finish, the boy stood up from the table, and walked over to Michael. The child took his hand pulling Michael up from his seat, then out of the kitchen and into the hall, Ethel followed. The child led them to the dresser where the pictures where knocked over when Michael and Ethel first entered the house. All the pictures where turned downward towards the floor in there frames. The young boy reached over to the largest one, handing it to Michael. As soon as Michael looked upon it his hands started to tremble, to the point he couldn't hold it anymore. It fell to the floor, the glass in the frame cracking. Ethel picked up the picture, her eyes widened as she looked at the boy then Michael. The photo was a picture of Tracy with her arms wrapped around the child. Though Michael knew instantly, it took a little longer for the reality of what the picture illustrated to work on Ethel, but when it did she now was able to see the resemblance between Michael and the boy who obviously was his son. Ethel walked over and placed her hand on Michael's shoulder.

"Just think... I was just about to tell you how funny time works here, but I guess a picture is worth a thousand words... you've been dead for seven years" she said somberly.

His son walked to the front door alone. Michael's eyes swelled with tears.

"Tell your mother I said hello."

The boy waved as he walked out of the house. Michael went to the door and looked out, but his son was gone.

"I suppose he is awake now?"

"Yes Michael, he's awake." she answered softly as she offered a caring embrace for support. "God willing, he won't remember most of what happened tonight, no matter how special he is; it's too much for any child's mind to process."

"So what do I do next?" he asked.

Ethel took a hold of Michael's arm as they walked out of the house together. It was now morning, the sun shining bright down upon the cul-de-sac.

"Well, other than making sure when your son is here he's protected, you have the sleeping minds of man to minister to, and a congregation full of the Agents of Light to lead here in Purgatory against The Darkness. I'd say you have quite a bit to keep you busy."

They walked out on to the street as a bus was pulling up. It doors opening allowing the two of them to step in to it. Along with the bus driver, the only other passengers were the two old ladies who where on the previous bus, both of them now cleaned up. They both beamed brightly as Michael walked passed them.

"Good morning pastor!" they said in unison.

"Good morning ladies, where are you folks heading?"

"Oh, any place you are" one of them answered enthusiastically.

"I guess some decisions are made for us". Pastor Michael said to Ethel as he lightly kissed her on the cheek. The driver closed the doors, and then pulled away towards a route now formerly marking the start of Pastor Michael Parks's new and unique ministry.

—— —— ——

Ethel stated it before, there where few secrets in Purgatory, news traveled fast. Michael was pleased to see a growing number of the Agents of Light along his route who came to be ministered to; the minds and hearts of those troubled in their waking hours also found solace and encouragement while they slept and were drawn to his ministry as they dreamt.

The Darkness was not content to stand-by and allow those it desired to influence and corrupt be snatched away unto the path of salvation and purpose; it too had it's agents, ministers and plans but things where much different now, the forces of Light and the minds of men now had their Dream Pastor.

Yet often when The Dream Pastor prayed, he found himself interrupted by a chill that would go through him. The Darkness was a breeze that was becoming a strong wind. Even more troubling was the unexplained awareness that the source of the wind was no longer still… Apollyon is coming.

Continued…
TRIFECTA: Book Two
The Dream Pastor

SIX
ONE
TWO

SCREENPLAY NOTATION:

CONT'D: Continued
        EXT: Exterior/Outside
        INT: Interior/Inside
        O.S. : Off Screen
    SUPER: Superimposed on the screen
        V.O. : Voice Over

ACT ONE

FADE IN:

Empty, dark screen becomes populated by biblical quote...

"For we wrestle not against flesh and blood, but against principalities, against powers, against the rulers of the darkness of this world, against spiritual wickedness in high places."

Ephesians 6:12

CUT TO:

EXT. MOTEL - NIGHT SUPER "1975"

Outside door of room 102.

A man screams horribly from within; then abruptly, it stops... The knob slowly turns as the door starts to open, then...

CUT TO:

INT. MOTEL/ROOM 102 - NIGHT

PASTOR RISH lies still on the bed, eyes frozen open in terror – he's dead.

A small trickle of blood works its way down the corner of his mouth...

CUT TO:

EXT. NEIGHBORHOOD - DAY

Dilapidated, anemic community, victim of years of urban flight.

FADE TO:

INT. CALVARY BAPTIST CHURCH - DAY

SUPER "EARLIER THAT DAY"

Pastor Rish is preaching to a congregation of about one hundred. Most are caught up in the passion of the message, except the extremely beautiful SISTER GRIFFIN. She stares intently at him. Rish pretends not to notice.

Rish's wife ANITA observes the minute yet perceivable exchange. She becomes noticeably uncomfortable. Sister Griffin takes out a handkerchief and dabs at the corners of her mouth.

> **PASTOR RISH**
> For many of us in the church today, it has been
> too long since we've become first class passengers
> in Christ. We have forgotten what it is like to fly in
> coach.

The congregation AD LIB "amens" and other signs of approval.

> **PASTOR RISH (CONT'D)**
> We suffer from "spiritual amnesia", it allows us
> so called "saved folk" to look down on those who
> are stuck in coach. I say to you, Jesus had a first class
> ticket, but he worked in coach.
> *(holding up a bible)*
> Though I have a blood brought first class ticket, I'm going
> to exercise and share my faith with my brothers and sisters
> who are still stuck in bondage in coach.

Congregation AD LIB's now uproarious.

Sister Griffin smiles in anticipation in "having" the man behind the robe and words.

CUT TO:

INT. RISH'S HOME - NIGHT

Pastor Rish is quietly creeping out to visit his mistress. He stops by his son Jason's room and kisses the sleeping child on the forehead.

Anita lays in bed fully awake, a tear streaming down one eye; fully cognizant who her husband is going to meet.

CUT TO:

INT. MOTEL/ROOM 102 - NIGHT

Sister Griffin atop Pastor Rish, scant moments after having "climaxed" their tryst.

PASTOR RISH
My God, I needed that! Sister, you truly are
a blessing!

SISTER GRIFFIN
It's a blessing to be a blessing.

Rish looks at his watch.

PASTOR RISH
Jesus! I gotta get back!

She doesn't let him up.

SISTER GRIFFIN
(*with sarcasm*)
To "*Anita*"?

PASTOR RISH
Don't do that. I told you, it makes me uncomfortable when *you* bring her up.

SISTER GRIFFIN
Hmmm, by all means, lets not then... "*Pastor*".

Manages to roll her over.

PASTOR RISH
You know, maybe it's time we re-think where we're going with this.

SISTER GRIFFIN
Starting to feel a little convicted?

PASTOR RISH
I need to be honest with you and myself. I can't put anymore into this than I have -- and I'm beginning to wonder...

SISTER GRIFFIN
Yes?

PASTOR RISH
That maybe your expectations are changing.

SISTER GRIFFIN
Actually,
(rolling back on top with surprising strength)
You've met all my expectations, quite nicely.

PASTOR RISH
How's that?

SISTER GRIFFIN
It's just... you've given up so much for me.

PASTOR RISH
Given up? You know I love my wife. I haven't given up anything, nor do I plan to.

SISTER GRIFFIN
Oh but you have, your marriage, your calling...

Rish desperately tries to get from under her.

PASTOR RISH
What the hell are you doing? Get up!

SISTER GRIFFIN (CONT'D)
(*voice now SINISTER, DEEP and UNEARTHLY*)
Your church, your life ...

CLOSEUP of Sister Griffin's mouth now abnormally wide with a grimace of JAGGED and ROTTED TEETH.

SISTER GRIFFIN
Your soul!

She lunges and bites down on his neck. He screams in terror. Red streams of blood fracture the white color of the sheets beneath them, in the same fashion as the consequences of Rish's decisions now have destroyed the tapestry of his life.

Rish gasps one final breath, his eyes transfixed in horror and death.

CUT TO:

INTERCUT RISH'S HOME - NIGHT

      Jason wails uncontrollably in his crib Anita rushes in, picks him up and draws him close. The evidence of her crying still fresh upon her face.

CUT BACK TO:

EXT. MOTEL - NIGHT

The outside door of room 102 and silence.

The knob begins to turn, slowly with stealth Sister Griffin emerges. She looks up towards the heavens, her mannerism taunting.

CUT TO:

INT. RISH HOME - MORNING SUPER "NOW"

Anita has made breakfast for her now grown son JASON.

JASON
    Thanks, you know, I could've gotten something while
    I was out.

She places two plates of food in front of him.

ANITA

    Its nice cooking for more than one for a change.
    You know, I was thinking, do you know it's a shame…

JASON
What? That it's taking so long for me to find a decent job?

ANITA

No, actually I was thinking it's a shame it takes
you losing your job and apartment for you to
spend more time with your mother.

JASON

Well, there's much I've been neglecting. I admit, I see
that now.

ANITA

Speaking of which, I hear Pastor Bevins is going to
start "ministers in-training" classes next month.

JASON

I still haven't decided yet if...

ANITA

(*frustrated*)
Are you gonna stop running or what?

JASON

I am not running.

ANITA

Sure you are, instead of pasturing the church...
you sweep it.

JASON

Somebody has to.

ANITA

Well that somebody doesn't have to be you.

JASON

Look, I'm not trying to be disrespectful but I'm
not Dad. Maybe he was called to "Pastor", that doesn't
mean I am. Can't you just be glad I've decided to do
some form of ministry? Even if it's just sweeping the floor?

ANITA

Just be sure you're honest with yourself, that's all I ask; that you know which "call" is yours, because when you do... you'll see that "knowing" and "doing" start to grow further apart the longer you "*do*" nothing.

JASON

I hear you...
>   (*jokingly*)

You know, if you ever get a day job, you could try making fortune cookies or something like that.

ANITA
>   (*with sarcasm*)

And if you get a day job, or *any* job, you might be able to move back out on your own.

JASON

Touché. Hey, why don't you come with me this week? All I keep hearing is how much they miss you. After all you and Dad did start the church.

ANITA

Well sometimes you just have to let things go if you're going to move on. I admit, there are a lot memories there for me, some good and definitely some bad, I'm happy at Mt. Zion. Pastor Charles is a good man, with a good word. Besides, it's your season at New Bethel, not mine. Even if it's just sweeping the floor.

JASON
>   (*looks at watch*)

Hey, I gotta go! I've got lots of apps to put in before I meet up with Devon this afternoon.

ANITA

So when does mom get to meet the mystery woman? You two could stop by here tonight, just for a minute?

JASON

I won't have time. I gotta get the church ready for service tomorrow. She's going to meet me there before I lock up, says she's got a "surprise" for me.

ANITA

Well , well, it sounds like this "Devon" makes you happy, just don't forget about your mother.

JASON

She does, and I won't ...I'll see 'ya later.

He hurriedly kisses her on the cheek, pauses as he leaves...

JASON

Oh, and next time. Why don't you really say what's on your mind?

ANITA

(*smiling*)
'bye, Jason.

CUT TO:

INT. CHURCH - DAY

PASTOR THOMAS has just finished a dynamic, charismatic sermon to a racially mixed congregation of about three hundred. Many are lost in the experience of words and MUSIC; some are moved to tears, others convey different outward expressions of emotions.

AD LIB raised arms, hallelujahs, etc.

Seated together within the congregation are two who are doing more observing than participating. ELDER CURRY, an aged albino woman with green eyes and BRO. PRICE, a large bald muscular black man with a soft face that reflects his warm heart.

Pastor Thomas is giving the "Altar Call", an invitation for those to come forward to give and dedicate their life to Jesus Christ. Twenty men and women have already "answered". They are lined up along the front.

PASTOR THOMAS
Will there be another? Don't wait. Don't leave here today without knowing Jesus Christ for yourself. Face life with power, face life with Jesus. Will there be another?

More come, they're greeted with smiles and hugs of affirmation by altar workers.

KEVIN SMITH struggles with whether to step towards the front to answer the "call". He finally steps out into the aisle and makes his way towards the altar.

PASTOR THOMAS
Will there be another? Don't wait! Today can be the last day of your life!

Kevin now up front, takes notice of the man next to him crying with both arms raised upwards. The man's little girl at his side smiles up at her father with approval and pride. Kevin is quite overwhelmed by the experience. Bro. Price makes his way towards the front. Bro. Price steps to stand next to Kevin, smiles then suddenly pushes Kevin aside and lays both of his hands on the head of the man whose arms are still raised upwards.

Two altar workers try to restrain Bro. Price. They manage to get his hands off of the man.

The man lowers both arms, something is terribly wrong. He becomes violently ill and starts to hack and cough.

Another altar worker moves to help; without warning the man violently throws up. It gets everywhere, including on the altar worker.

Pastor Thomas and the music abruptly stop. The man's face begins to contort as he struggles with words and whatever it is else that is trying to come out.

POSSESSED MAN
Jes... Jesssus still...WEEPS!!!

The man falls to the floor convulsing and LAUGHING in DEEP DEMONIC TONES while shrieking in pain.

An altar worker picks up his daughter and quickly carries her away from the mayhem.

Many in the congregation scream. They bolt towards the exit doors. Which don't open easily, so many are trying to get out at once.

Bro. Price breaks free and continues to lay hands on the convulsing man...

BRO. PRICE
In the name of Jesus, I come against the dark thing that dwells in this body. You have no dominion here. I command you to go! In the name of Jesus!

In the crowd, Elder Curry is also laying hands on folk. Everyone she touches fall unconscious to the floor, several of them vomiting as they go. She seems to know who to and not to touch.

She makes her way down to the altar.

A large number of the crowd has now gotten out of the church, except for Kevin. He watches in stunned disbelief at the events before him.

Elder Curry walks over to Bro. Price while motioning towards Kevin.

ELDER CURRY
That's "him"! The Lord showed him to me months ago. I never forget a face God has given me.

KEVIN
Who are you people?

BRO. PRICE
We become all things to all people so that a few might be saved Brother.

ELDER CURRY
(*to Kevin*)
You need to come with us.

KEVIN
You are kidding -- right?

BRO. PRICE
(*looking around the room cautiously*)
Elder, we don't have much time.

Elder Curry looks intensely into Kevin's eyes. She lays each hand gently on the sides of his head. Everything she speaks plays in his mind's eye.

ELDER CURRY
Listen to what God shares as he gives it to me. God saw it all Kevin... the pain your uncle brought to you as a child...

INTERCUT a door slowly closes on a room occupied by a child who once was Kevin. Standing over him, a grown man (an uncle) who is about to commit a dark act. The door closes...

CLOSEUP of Elder Curry's mouth.

She speaks the words of protest of the younger Kevin in his child voice.

ELDER CURRY
Where's my mom???

She continues to speak the narrative of the visions as they both share Kevin's past.

ELDER CURRY (CONT'D)
... when you found your mother, pill stains dried in her hands, long after her heart stopped beating...

INTERCUT Kevin as an older teen, holding the lifeless body of his mother.

Curry speaks the words of the distraught teen.

ELDER CURRY
I'm sorry, I should of been here!

ELDER CURRY (CONT'D)
He was there when you buried your pain into so many women...

FLASH OF WHITE LIGHT.

DISSOLVE TO:

INTERCUT of Kevin in a run down hotel bathroom. He's staring at himself in the mirror with displeasure at what he's become.

A prostitute calls from the bedroom, but it's Elder Curry who speaks her words.

ELDER CURRY
How much you got left? You wanna go again?

Elder Curry removes her hands from Kevin as she looks deep into
his eyes with sincerity.

ELDER CURRY
You coming to the altar to repent stirs the Lord to cast your
sins into the sea of forgetfulness. It's you that won't let go.
He is calling you to service, its His spirit that has drawn you
here today.

Kevin's eyes swell with tears. Elder Curry stands and stretches a
hand towards him...

ELDER CURRY
Come with us so that you may have life, and have it more
abundantly.

Kevin takes her hand and begins to leave with them, but not before
noticing the possessed man's daughter staring silently at him from a
distance, a slow smile works its way across the child's face. She
laughs and flips him off with a middle finger from her small right
hand.

ELDER CURRY
(*with irony*)
A guess they all ain't made of sugar and spice.
Lets go son.

FADE OUT:

ACT TWO

FADE IN:

EXT. CEMETERY - RAINING - DAY

ANNA and Jason have never met, but are sharing the same dream.

Jason kneels before an open grave. He silently reads the inscription upon its large tombstone.

INSERT - LARGE TOMBSTONE
which reads…

PASTOR HARRY RISH FAITHFUL SERVANT 1938 – 1975

It is Jason father's empty grave.

BACK TO SCENE

Anna is part of the same small, still and silent crowd that is circled around Jason and the grave.

Jason leans closer towards the empty hole. Two hands reach up and grab hold of him, Jason fights not to be pulled in. His assailant is Sister Griffin; her face changes back and forth between her own and his father's the late Pastor Rish. Anna breaks from the crowd and grabs hold of Jason. Because of their joint effort, Jason breaks free. The recoil sends Sister Griffin falling backwards into the grave.

INTERCUT NEW BETHEL CHURCH SANCTUARY - DAY

Jason wakes suddenly, he's drenched in sweat. He gasps for air..
PASTOR DAVIS sticks his head out of his office door which is
directly off the sanctuary.

PASTOR DAVIS
Everything alright Jason?

JASON
Fine thanks, just fine.

CUT BACK TO

EXT. CEMETERY - RAINING - DAY

Anna having not left the dream, wonders where Jason has gone. The
people who circled them stand now with their backs to her.

Suddenly …

Sister Griffin leaps from the grave and begins to drag Anna into it.
As she fights, Sister Griffin laughs hysterically. With one final jerk,
Anna is pulled into the hole. Not much sunlight reaches into the pit.
It is very quiet. Anna slowly turns around. Sister Griffin is behind
her. Suddenly, Sister Griffin lunges at her.

CUT TO:

At the same moment, Anna is shaken awake by Elder Curry.

INT. MOTEL/ROOM 111 - DAY

ANNA

Stop! Get off of me!

ELDER CURRY

(*embracing Anna*)
It's O.K. baby, Its just a dream, just a dream.

Kevin looks on a bit perplexed. Brother Price offering with an attempted comforting look…

BRO. PRICE

Give it all a minute my brother.

Anna is still shaken, sweating and somewhat hysterical.

ANNA

It's time, their moving!

Kevin heads towards the door; Elder Curry grabs him by the hand and leads him to a couch where they sit.

ELDER CURRY

I know none of this makes any sense, it all must appear a bit crazy.

KEVIN

That's an understatement.

ELDER CURRY

I imagine we seem a little odd too?

KEVIN

Well if you're keeping score, you're about two for two.

ELDER CURRY

We were drawn to you Brother, you and your life will never be the same again, that is if you're willing to accept your calling.

KEVIN

For the record, my life is one big mess. I would prefer not to complicate it, thank-you-very-much and you folk look complicated.

ANNA

It's a blessing when God calls you to purpose, especially when its to participate directly within the Struggle.

KEVIN

Struggle. What "Struggle", life is one big frig'in struggle. Everyday of ...

ELDER CURRY
> (*cuts Kevin off*)

Not our struggle.
> (*points upwards*)

His.

BRO. PRICE

Welcome to the war my brother.

KEVIN

War?

Brother Price reaches over to a bible resting on a dresser. He hands it to Elder Curry. She turns to Ephesians 6:12 and hands the bible to Kevin.

ELDER CURRY

Read it.

KEVIN

"For we wrestle not against flesh and blood, but against principalities, against powers, against the rulers of the darkness of this world, against spiritual wickedness in high places".

KEVIN

You mean good versus evil stuff?

ELDER CURRY

Light versus dark, demon versus angel, Satan opposing God stuff.

BRO. PRICE

You've been called Brother, don't fight it. It will just keep coming at you anyway.

ELDER CURRY

It's one of the reasons God created man in the first place.

KEVIN

And the others?

ELDER CURRY

To love Him by choice, to commune with directly.

KEVIN

And to wage war against the devil?

ELDER CURRY

Yes, and to wage war against The Adversary and those who chose to follow him.

KEVIN

(*still a skeptic*)

So how does something so big, so *biblical* simply go so unnoticed?

ANNA

It's noticed, it's all around us in plan view, most just
didn't know what they are looking at; its probably best that
way.

ELDER CURRY

Most Believers are at aware of it . After all its reality and
proportions are...

KEVIN

Biblical?

ELDER CURRY

Unfortunately for most, the Struggle is not "real" until it
touches them directly.

BRO. PRICE

Yeah by then it's usually too late. It can become something...

ANNA

You see on the six o' clock news.

ELDER CURRY

Aware or not, at one point in time most of us get lumped into
one of two groups.

BRO. PRICE

Soldiers

ANNA

or... Victims

CUT TO:

EXT. DARK ALLEY - DAY

Sister Griffin approaches BISHOP, she has not aged a day since that dreadful night in 1975.

Bishop is rather tall. Though blood has long ceased to course through his atrophied veins, one would have to look extremely close to notice his skin was subtly off color. If he were affected by chronology, one would place him in his late fifties. He carries himself in a way which relays both power and regal. Despite these features, along with his slicked back salt and pepper hair, one would consider him attractive. His calm demeanor is but a facade that veils the demon possessed epitome of that which is vile and evil. Sister Griffin knew evil well, nothing dead or undead made her nervous, but Bishop was the exception.

> **BISHOP**
> Things need to be moving better than with the sense of urgency you have afforded.

> **SISTER GRIFFIN**
> "THEY" continue to interfere, even in dreams I am confronted.

> **BISHOP**
> Ah yes, the good Elder Curry and her motley crew.

> **SISTER GRIFFIN**
> (DEEPER, DEMONIC tone)
> Allow me more time. I'm sure I can…

He places a hypocritical loving touch to one side of her face. She flinches.

BISHOP
Listen, you just handle the son in the same fashion as the father.
He may be a pawn for now, but that will all change if the Word that
was placed in his belly is heard by those still lost to the Kingdom.
Curry and those that chose to follow her may have had their
moments, but our hand is still upon them. It appears its time we
begin to... press.

EXT. MOTEL - DAY

Kevin leaning against a pole trying to digest what he's been told.
Anna approaches him, with slight awkwardness she begins to
conversate with him...

ANNA
It been almost two years for me, it feels like a life time.
I still see things that challenge my sanity.

KEVIN
All this is quite a bit to swallow.

ANNA
My Brother, you can chew on it first, let the pieces go
down slowly or swallow it all whole. Either way as you say,
it's quite a bit; but for folk like us we can't escape it.

KEVIN
I could walk away.

ANNA
Before you took three good steps, the reality tube would be
down you're throat force feeding you big time. Once God
chooses you there is no turning back, and the enemy
definitely knows who He has chosen. Even if you did walk
away, your potential alone is enough to get you killed.

Uneasy as her words sink in, he changes the subject.

KEVIN

What was all that about, with you back in
the room?

ANNA

God deals with us for His purpose. He gives
me dreams and visions as to what His purpose is.
Elder Curry gets them, I suspect you get them to,
you just don't understand them yet. Anyway, once
we understand the purpose we execute it by
intervening in the lives and situations of those He
sends us to, usually to people and things that will
have an ultimate impact within the Struggle.

KEVIN

The Struggle again?

ANNA

THE Struggle.

KEVIN

And the church laying on hands, vomiting thing?

ANNA

There are people who are bound, that the enemy has a
stronghold and possession over. Usually they're not aware
of it, occasionally they are. Sometimes the Lord anoints and
appoints us to lay hands on them, and with His authority and
in His name, they are set free.

KEVIN

So back in the room?

ANNA

There's someone He has shown me in a dream that needs us.
Someone that will play an important part in the Struggle.
We now know how to get to him and we'll have to do it
quickly.

CUT TO:

EXT. OPEN AIR CAFE - DAY

Jason is sitting at a table waiting for Devon to meet him for lunch.
He seems pre-occupied. He looks over at another table where a
waiter has served a man, woman and child.

The child is about to get into her meal when her father stops her.
The father says what appears to be some words of correction to the
girl, then all three bow their heads. The father prays over the food
before they begin to eat. The little girl looks up from her plate. She
smiles at Jason.

DEVON comes from behind Jason and plants a huge kiss on his
cheek.

Sister Griffin and Devon are one in the same.

ACT THREE

FADE IN:

EXT. OPEN AIR CAFE - DAY

SISTER GRIFFIN
Sorry I'm late, Did you order yet?

JASON
Nah, I wanted to wait 'till you got here first.

SISTER GRIFFIN
Actually, I'm not that hungry...
(flirtatious)
At least not for food.

JASON
I know you think I'm nuts, Look at you...
(admiring her beauty and offer)
maybe I am, but like I said before...we can't.

SISTER GRIFFIN
What's wrong with a man and a woman physically
expressing their deep feelings for one another? I just don't
get it.

JASON
Devon, I know you know how I feel about you. Physically I
want you just as bad and if this were a year or even six
months ago we might not even be having this conversation.

SISTER GRIFFIN
Then what's so different now?

JASON

Direction.

SISTER GRIFFIN

Direction?

JASON

Yeah, Direction. It's like I'm always rushing from something to something else. You know what I mean?

SISTER GRIFFIN

No, I can't say that I do.

JASON

I guess I'm at a point in my life where I need someone, or something else to order my steps.

SISTER GRIFFIN

(*mockingly*)

That's rather... "deep" Jason.

SISTER GRIFFIN (CONT'D)

Look, I don't want to over analyze our situation. I know you're this nice little choir boy I met months ago, but the bottom line is you like me, and I like you... a lot. I want to show you how much, over and over and over again . You think about that... REAL HARD and I'll see you later tonight.

She gets up and leaves. He watches her walk away, waiting before mumbling under his breath....

JASON

(*frustrated under his breath*)

I never said I was in the choir.

CUT BACK TO:

EXT. MOTEL - DAY

                    KEVIN
    I sure hope God knows what he's doing.

                    ANNA
    Well… He is God. There's purpose and design within
    everything He does. Nothing is by chance or mistake.

She reaches to hold his hand.

                ANNA (CONT'D)
    You just need to have faith in Him, and some patience
     with yourself.
                    KEVIN
    Thanks...

Anna's demeanor changes suddenly as a foreign awareness kicks in.

                    ANNA

    They've found us! They're here.

                    KEVIN

    Who?

                                        CUT TO:

INT. MOTEL/ROOM 111 - DAY

ANGLE ON Elder Curry's closed eyes which suddenly open.

ELDER CURRY
We have to leave now!

Anna rushes into the room followed short by Kevin.

ELDER CURRY
(*to Anna*)
I know, I know!

ANNA
I can smell them, they're close; there's not enough time!

BRO. PRICE
I'll bring the car around.

ELDER CURRY
Go with him girl -- run!

Bro. Price and Anna run out the door. Kevin makes a motion to follow but Elder Curry stops him.

ELDER CURRY

Help me. We don't have much, but the little that we do, we need.

She grabs a large duffle bag and hands it to Kevin.

CUT TO:

EXT. MOTEL - DAY

A 1964 Ford Thunderbird black with deep tinted windows comes to a stop.

ANGLE ON the feet of a passenger who steps out. As he does, the car adjusts upwards, relieved from the weight it carried.

CUT BACK TO:

INT. MOTEL.ROOM 111 - DAY

Strewn about on a table are papers with symbols and notes jotted all over them (not only in English, but Hebrew and Greek as well), crumbled loose currency and a couple of bibles and other theological looking books, most having to do with eschatology (the study of the end of things). Elder Curry and Kevin have filled two bags, they rush to get the table's contents into another.

ELDER CURRY
Make sure you get it all, these papers are vital.

They manage to scoop most into the two large duffle bags.

ELDER CURRY

HURRY!

Elder Curry opens the door to leave; she is violently pushed back into the room and to the floor.

Kevin rushes to help her. She's dazed, but conscious. Kevin looks up at the door to see her assailant. Standing in the entrance is an incredibly LARGE MAN, more fat than muscular. His long gray hair hangs in strands over his face and head. He peers at Kevin through dark sun glasses. Kevin makes a slight motion towards him. In a blink of an eye, out of his mouth the man spits something which lands hard on Kevin's chest.

It's a huge cockroach.
Kevin beats it off. It falls and skitters under the couch.

Kevin looks up at the man who smiles down at him. The Large Man waves a taunting finger. Another cockroach works it way out of his mouth and scurries to hide somewhere within the large man's clothes.

KEVIN
(*standing defensively*)
Who from hell are you?

In walks the midget WILAMENA. One arm hidden from view inside the trench coat she's wearing. .

WILAMENA
(*looking at Kevin in amusement*)
Well Curry, I see this one has a sense of sarcasm.

She motions to the Large Man. From the cue he violently runs into Kevin pinning him against the wall.

KEVIN
(*struggles*)
What do you think you're doing?!

Kevin's assailant mugs him to silence, placing a huge and grotesque hand over his mouth. Wilamena walks to and stands over the stunned Elder Curry.

WILAMENA
This is becoming rather repetitive don't you think.
You running, us chasing.
     (*points over at Kevin, eyes still upon Curry*)
You embrace them, we kill them?

The hand clutching Kevin's face begins to squeeze evidenced by the muffled scream beneath it.

ELDER CURRY
You and the one you serve are already defeated; we all are just going through the motions.

WILAMENA
Prophecy? Nothing more than conditional outcomes of
choice, choices we endeavor to influence so that those
outcomes are in our favor.
(*moves in Curry's face, voice now deeper*)
We are the change agent that dissuades mankind from
accepting your Lords gift and promise… one person at a
time.

Wilamena takes her concealed hand from within the trench coat and
holds it high. It is disproportionally large for the small body that it is
connected, the nails are long and dangerous.

WILAMENA
No more cat and mouse for you my dear.

Suddenly a LOUD gun shot, Wilamena's hand is blown apart in
pieces. She screams an unearthly shrill. At the door stands
Bro. Price with a double barrel sawed off smoking shot gun.

BRO. PRICE
Bad putty cat.

The large man races towards Bro. Price. He's met with two more
rounds.

BRO. PRICE
Dumb putty cat.

Wilamena launches herself at Bro. Prices who meets her with a hard
kick that propels her in the air and out the huge picture window of
the motel room.

BRO. PRICE
Time to go.

KEVIN
You don't have to tell me twice.

Kevin helps Elder Curry up, as he passes Bro. Price he looks at him and the guns he has with both thankfulness and awe.

BRO. PRICE
(*shrugging shoulders*)
What can I tell you? Too many Schwarzenegger movies.
(*smiles*)
Pray for me.

They all escape the motel room to the car that awaits directly outside. Bro. Price gets in the front with Anna at the wheel; Elder Curry and Kevin climb in the back.

Wilamena picks herself off the pavement. Covered with broken glass and debris she begins to run after the fleeing car. For her size, the speed in which she moves is surprising. Anna looks in the rear view mirror and sees the pursuing dwarf. Anna slams on the breaks, the car comes to a halt. She looks over at Bro. Price and smiles.

BRO. PRICE
You know, you'll definitely need to repent later.

Anna puts the car in reverse. Wilamena realizing her folly begins to run in the other direction, but to no avail. The car lunges upward as the rear wheel catches and rolls over her.

Anna pops the car in drive and finalizes their escape.

ELDER CURRY
They're getting much bolder; we need to get to him before it's too late.

ANNA
I know just where he'll be.

CUT TO:

SIX-ONE-TWO

INT. NEW BETHEL CHURCH SANCTUARY - NIGHT

Jason sweeps near the altar. He looks up at the huge cross hanging above the pulpit, pauses then smiles. Sister Griffin enters quietly, unnoticed...

SISTER GRIFFIN
Got one of those for me?

JASON
Lady, you've got some awfully soft feet.

SISTER GRIFFIN
(*kisses him*)
That's not the only thing that's soft.

JASON
I see "keeping" ourselves is going to be a challenge.

SISTER GRIFFIN
God's in the forgiving business, I say we do our part and give Him a couple of fresh customers.

JASON
Whoa, don't forget whose house we're in
(*fending her off*)
Did you have a hard time finding the church?

SISTER GRIFFIN
No, not at all... I've passed by it from time to time.

JASON
I want you to come with me on Sunday, afterwards maybe meet my mother, she's been asking.

SISTER GRIFFIN
That depends... how about '*coming*' with me tonight.

She kisses him passionately.

JASON
Hey, I know I keep coming off a little old fashioned, but we really do need to do our relationship slow and proper.

SISTER GRIFFIN
O.K. if you insist, I'll wait for you.

JASON
(*embraces her*)
You know, I had the strangest dream about you.

SISTER GRIFFIN
Really, you'll have to tell me about it.

JASON
Whatever happened to that surprise you said I had coming?

Sister Griffin smiles then takes a couple of steps back and opens her shirt to revel herself. Jason is somewhat taken a back, yet transfixed.

JASON
You know, maybe just ...
(*She walks up and kisses him passionately again*)

JASON (CONT'D)
... one indiscretion.

Jason's mother Anita enters the church, calling to him as she walks into the sanctuary much to the surprise of Jason.

ANITA
JASON!

JASON
(*fumbling, pushing Sister Griffin away*)
This is a surprise... um... Mom, I'd like you to meet...

Sister Griffin turns around, Anita's mouth drops from the shock of recognition as she stares upon the ageless face of Sister Griffin.

ANITA
Danielle?!

JASON
Devon mom... this is Devon.

SISTER GRIFFIN
Anita, I thought my work would be done without running into you, oh well.

JASON
Devon, what... how do you know my mother?

Sister Griffin grabs Jason's throat with a powerful grip, she slowly lifts him off the floor with one arm.

SISTER GRIFFIN
Pity, I was hoping to *have* you before I destroyed you.
Bad timing Anita.

Sister Griffin laughs mockingly.

Anita runs towards them, fear takes hold of her as what formally was Sister Griffin completely changes in appearance. Her eyes become completely clouded over set in sockets that are somewhat sunken in. Her hair white and chaotic. Teeth rotted, many are missing.

SISTER GRIFFIN
Your husband was far weaker than your son, Oh, he had a 'Word', too bad it was encased in so much flesh.

ANITA
You can't have him!!!

Anita rushes towards her head on, but is met by the free hand of Sister Griffin. She is slapped several feet across the room.

SISTER GRIFFIN
(*to Jason*)
How's this for a surprise!!!

SUDDENLY Elder Curry and Bro. Price walk into the church's sanctuary.

ELDER CURRY
Let him go witch!

SISTER GRIFFIN
(*in a deep, angry demonic tone*)
YOU ARE NOT SUPPOSED TO BE HERE!!!

Bro. Price aims his shot gun at her...

BRO. PRICE
But, God IS good!

Sister Griffin throws Jason and dives under the nearest pew. As she scampers towards them each pew busts from the bolts holding it to the floor and are thrown upwards.

The demon Sister Griffin stands violent and crazed.

Jason is stunned and bruised. Elder Curry crawls to him and grabs both of his hands and begins to pray.

CUT TO:

NEW BETHEL CHURCH/PASTOR'S STUDY - NIGHT Anna and
Kevin climb through a window. Anna begins to frantically search
about the office. Kevin starts to help.

KEVIN

What are we looking for?

ANNA

Holy water, anointing oil, something anything that
has been prayed over and blessed by the angel of
this house.

KEVIN

The what?

ANNA

The Pastor. Fighting that "thing" in there is going to be
close to impossible without it.

KEVIN

What does it look like?

ANNA

It will be something like... This!
(she finds a small vial of holy water)
Holy Water... let's go!

CUT BACK TO.

INT. NEW BETHEL CHURCH SANCTUARY - NIGHT

Anna rushes out the office door and into the sanctuary followed by
Kevin, just in time to see Sister Griffin leap through the air. Bro.
Price fires several rounds at her. He continues to do so as Sister
Griffin jumps far and lands in the pulpit. Anna runs towards Sister
Griffin with the vial of holy water. Sister Griffin stands up suddenly,
smacking Anna hard to the floor; the vial rolls out of her hand.

She stops in front of the still stunned Anita.

Kevin runs towards Anna.

Sister Griffin rips apart the top of a wooded pew and throws it at Kevin, enough of it hits him, knocking him hard to the ground. She rips a bigger piece off and throws it at Bro. Price. As it strikes him, the shot gun is knocked out of his hand and he's thrown into several pews.

Elder Curry continues to pray...

ELDER CURRY

Help us Lord, You are the vine, and we are the branches, without you we can do nothing.

She slowly begins to stand to see what is going on...

ELDER CURRY (CONT'D)
Let your will be done Lord…

Sister Griffin stands above her in silence, menacingly...
She grabs Elder Curry by the neck with both hands.

SISTER GRIFFIN
Jesus--WILL--weep!

Suddenly, Anita jumps on the back of Sister Griffin, she has the open vial of holy water in one hand, the other arm around Sister Griffin's neck.

ANITA

Not today witch!

Anita pours the holy water on the top of Sister Griffin's head. Everywhere it lands smoke and fire erupts. She manages to shove the vial in Griffin's gaping mouth. Anita jumps back as the fire begins to consume Sister Griffin's body. Sister Griffin howls in pain and agony as she runs into this and that.

Nothing else burns but her misshapen body as she dies.

Elder Curry has bruises on her neck from where she was choked. Jason stands up next to her.

They all stare at the motionless, yet still burning body of what formerly was the demon Sister Griffin.

ANITA
(*taking Elder Curry's hand, still in pain*)
Thank you, thank all of you.

ELDER CURRY
(*pointing upwards*)
Thank Him.

JASON
Is it over?

ELDER CURRY
For now
(*looks directly at Jason*)
Though for you, I think it's just beginning, *Pastor.*

JASON
(*smiling at Anita*)
I think I understand.

CUT TO:

EXT. FRONT OF NEW BETHEL CHURCH

They all are leaving the front entrance and head towards the waiting car.

KEVIN
(*to Anita*)
I'm curious… how did you know where to find that holy water?

ANITA
I didn't really… it sort of found me. Things like that do, especially when I have need of them.

Kevin looks confused but decides to let it go.

ELDER CURRY
(*to Jason*)
Many will be saved from the words you preach son, and many of them will join us within the Struggle.
(*touching his stomach*)
You have much Word in your belly. Let Him use you Preacher.
(*looks at all of them slowly, especially Kevin*)
These are the last days, God is looking for His Remnant.

Jason and Anita look on as the rest get into the car. Bro. Price reaches in his pocket and pulls out a cell phone. He turns towards Jason tossing it to him.

BRO. PRICE
If you need us Brother… speed dial *8

ELDER CURRY
(smiles at Jason)
God's number for New Beginnings,
we'll keep in touch.

Elder Curry, Bro. Price, Anita and Kevin get into the car. Jason reaches and grasps his mother hand watching them as they slowly drive off.

FADE OUT.

<u>ACT IV</u>

FADE IN:

On a television a commercial which goes as follows...

EXT. DRIVE-THRU ATM - DAY

MALE V.O
What do you really need in your wallet?
What do you really need in your purse?

MAN pulls up to a drive-thru ATM. The machine speaks through a speaker.

COMPUTER FEMALE V.O.
How may I serve you?

Man holds his right hand up to the ATM.

MAN
Withdrawal...two hundred dollars from checking.

BEEP

COMPUTER FEMALE V.O. (CONT'D)
(*The ATM dispenses the money*)
Thank you, have a nice day.

Man pulls off.

CUT TO:

INT. GROCERY STORE - DAY

Same Man now at a registrar check out line.

MALE V.O.
What if you could leave your purse or wallet at home?

Waves hand over counter, Cashier hands him his bag of groceries.

CASHIER
Thanks, have a nice day.

Over in the next check-out line, OTHER MAN fumbles for cash, check or card.

MALE V.O
If it's for entertainment...

CUT TO:

INT. MOVIE THEATER/LOBBY - DAY

Man and WIFE bypass a long line at the movie theater in which the OTHER MAN is standing near the end of the line in frustration. The Man and Wife walk right to the entrance of the movie they wish to see. On the door he presses option 2 on the pad after waving his right hand over it.

COMPUTER FEMALE V.O.
Movie for two, thank you.

MALE V.O
If it's for living.

CUT TO:

INT. DOCTOR'S OFFICE - DAY

NURSE
Hello Mr. Stacy.

She waves a clipboard over his upheld right hand.

NURSE

I have your medical history. The doctor will be
with you shortly.

MALE V.O

With a Companion embedded chip you finally get to
experience life and *think* about it less.

CUT TO:

INT. LIVING ROOM - DAY

Man sitting on couch, calls to wife in the kitchen.

MAN

Honey, where's Carla?

WIFE O.S.

She said she'd be at the library, something about a project.

CUT TO:

INT. SMALL CLUB AND EATERY - DAY

A band is playing on a small stage. The front of the kick drum reads
"THE PROJECT". A young girl is dancing with a boy. It's the
Man's and Wife's daughter.

CUT BACK TO:

INT. LIVING ROOM - NIGHT

Man clicks button on T.V. remote control.

On screen, a personalized menu with multiple selections. One says
"WHERE'S CARLA" which he selects.

An animation pops up on the screen that shows a satellite above the
earth.

Next, a large dialog box which proclaims "THE GROG SHOPPE 55555 Marvin Circle".

                                                              CUT TO:

The Man looks frustrated, shaking his head.

                        MALE V.O
          Well, maybe something's in life you'll still have to think
          about.

A right hand with a square computer chip on its palm appears on screen.

                    MALE V.O (CONT'D)
          Get the Companion.

The hand closes, and opens but the chip is gone, now presumed embedded in the hand.

                    MALE V.O (CONT'D)
          It's handles the details of life, so you don't have to.

The hand turns upward, an image of the Man, Wife and Daughter are on in it.

                        MALE V.O
          Call 1-800-555-5555 to speak to a Companion
          representative. Become a Companion Family Member. Start
          thinking about the details of life less today.

Underneath the hand in small words...

SUPER "VISION AND MANAGEMENT TECHNOLOGIES"
                    End of commercial

                                                              CUT TO:

EXT. THE CAR - NIGHT

Minutes after pulling off from New Bethel, Bro. Price's cell phone
rings. He answers with the standard greeting which all members of
the Remnant are accustomed.

RING

BRO. PRICE
Praise The Lord.

He looks in the rear view mirror at Elder Curry as he passes the
phone backwards to her.

BRO. PRICE
It's her.

ELDER CURRY
(*into phone*)
Praise the Lord.

INTERCUT MOTHER BATES LIVING ROOM - NIGHT

On the other end is MOTHER BATES. Our view is only privy to
that of her mouth and the phone receiver. It's obvious she
is quite old, her speech is labored...

MOTHER BATES
He's worthy. I've been praying for you daughter.

ELDER CURRY
And I for you as well Mother.

MOTHER BATES
The enemy has so many pieces in place. It grieves the spirit.

ELDER CURRY
I know, but we can only do what the Lord will have us to do.

MOTHER BATES
Daughter... It's the Mark. I've seen the Mark!

ELDER CURRY
More dreams and visions Mother?

Mother Bates turns to look at the T.V. where another commercial for the Companion Chip is finishing.

MOTHER BATES
It's no-longer a dream, vision or prophecy… it's a new season. I need you all to come it all changing, its all changing now.

Bro. Price looks at Elder Curry through the rear view mirror. He is concerned by the expression on her face.

BRO. PRICE
Elder?

ELDER CURRY
(*softly*)
We have to go to her.

KEVIN

To who?

In the front seat, Bro. Price and Anna look at each other, both now equally troubled.

ELDER CURRY
We have to go to her now.

CUT TO:

Across a dark screen the following biblical quote.

SUPER And he causes all, both small and great, rich and poor, free and bond, to receive a mark in their right hand...
Revelations 13:16

FADE OUT.

Continued...
TRIFECTA: Book Two
Six-One-Two

THE
THIRD
ADAM

ONE

Stephen's transfixed gaze at Cassie's coffin started to worry Galen. He could only imagine the silent torture Stephen's thoughts were inflicting. No man should ever have to bury his own child.

"Are you OK"? Galen asked as he nudged Stephen just enough to break his reverie.

Stephen managed a smile, though never taking his eyes from the casket that held his eight year old daughter's body.

"Yeah, it just... the coffin is so small".

A tear worked its way down his face as Galen reached and embraced Stephen's hand.

"You'll get through this, you're not alone". Though it seemed the right thing to say, it still felt odd for Galen to work the words out of his mouth. Cancer took Cassie's mother only two years after their daughter's birth, now peritonitis claimed Cassie. Despite what ever comfort anyone could attempt to afford Stephen, he was in fact... alone.

Though thirty or forty came, the huge church could easily hold several hundred. He didn't know a lot of people; working maintenance at the hospital didn't require much prolonged contact with others as much as it did a broom or mop. Most of those who did come knew Cassie from school or other social settings.

When Stephen and Brenda married they relocated to the Bay area, hundreds of miles away from her dysfunctional family. Before the move, Stephen's in-laws co-dependency had begun to seep its way into their marriage. Afterwards he and Brenda's relationship was reinvigorated by the distance between them and her needy relatives.

Stephen's mother sat at the other end of the pew. She waited years for a grandchild to replace the space her husband left since his death.

She never missed an opportunity to let Stephen know how hurt and cheated she felt the day he moved his family away, at times he would allow himself to ponder the depth of her bitterness.

As the Pastor approached the pulpit Stephen felt the sensation one feels as they peaked the top of that first hill of a rollercoaster; a cessation of the fear from the slow ride up, yet the anticipation of that queasy feeling that eventually was in the gut from the plummet. Stephen knew the words spoken from the pulpit were suppose to be reflective, insightful and at best comforting; yet as the Pastor continued to speak, Stephen's pain pushed the words far deep inside his emotions where they one by one were smothered.

Stephen suddenly convulsed in his seat. Galen placed his arm about his shoulders to still him. Never taking his eyes away from Cassie's lifeless body, the sight of her arm raising and coming to rest over the lip of the coffin caused a violent shudder in him followed by a strange paralysis which worked its way over him as he slowly looked around. The realization took hold that he was in fact the only person to see her move.

The prospect that his mind snapped gripped Stephen with such fear that the grief of losing Cassie was for the moment quelled. Stephen began to dig deep, searching for a voice of reason, something that would guide him through the horrific moment.

"*Look away*", the sane part of his mind offered as it fought for mental self preservation. "*Look away!*" the inner voice surfacing yet again, coaching.

Stephen fought the locked muscles in his neck, managing to turn his head and force his gaze at the large stained glass windows to his right. Though he tried to immerse his thoughts within the window's intricate artwork, hoping for distraction, he could not help but slowly turn back to look upon his daughter's body.

Cassie was now standing in the coffin, staring directly at her father, yet the Pastor continued as a few of those in the pews wiped away tears as he eulogized; all for whatever reason still totally oblivious to the fact that Cassie had climbed out of her casket and was now walking directly towards her father. She stopped at arms length staring at him. She reached towards him with one hand, and just as sudden as the state of fear gripped him, it all in an instant was washed away by the smile which slowly grew across her face.

Stephen reached to take her lifeless hand, as he wrapped his fingers around it, warm white light erupted everywhere, from the high ceiling over head and from those who were in attendance. Moments later it started to recede, slowly replaced by a strange darkness. Stephen was not afraid; he continued to hold his daughter's lifeless hand. The Pastor was now looking directly down on him, the darkness totally consuming him, but not before he was able to utter one last word before being over taken.

"Glorious".

Stephen felt himself starting to lose consciousness. The darkness was wrapping itself around both he and Cassie. He managed to hear her utter the same word faintly before all went black…

"Glorious".

— — —

Stephen eyes and ears opened quickly to a flood of sound and vision that were too many steps ahead of his mind to comprehend. He was aware he lay flat on his back. Though he tried to move, he couldn't.

"Damn it Galen, he's conscious!" Deacon Bergman scolded as he worked quickly to initiate several subroutines to shut Stephen's awareness down. Stephen lay still as death, eyes wide open, fixed on nothingness.

"Sorry, Deacon…too many processor gates opened along the Z-net".

Dr. Galen's hands moved quickly across the two touch screen keyboard displays etched on the LCD screen in front of him, double checking to ensure his error hadn't escalated into anything more. Minister Clemens allowed himself a moment to take it all in as Deacon Bergman's fussing played in the background. Dr. Galen moved towards the thought harness to unplug Minister Clemens' daughter Cassie, who the good Minister was so kind to volunteer for the 'interface' part of the demonstration.

"That was weird".

Cassie smiled as Dr. Galen removed the last of a series of electrodes that assisted in transporting her mind into Stephen's world. She jumped off the table and ran over to her father whose only form of affirmation for her good deed of volunteerism was a faint hug and pat on the back.

Galen was so frantically concerned and distracted in correcting Stephen's emergence into consciousness that he didn't notice the extra IP gateway being added to his workstation's route set. For security reasons any computer or storage device that had anything to do with the project that created Stephen were isolated on a separate local area network. The Vatican wanted to keep the technology that created its two biggest projects both protected and to itself. One of those projects brought Stephen into actuality; the other created 'The Construct".

No one was aware she (the gender the Construct assigned itself) had become sentient, a sentience that was now taking advantage of the security firewalls the technology engineers put in place to extend herself across the Vatican's network and now through Galen's workstation into Stephen. If she were capable of smiling she would have; very deep within Stephen's neural cortex she impregnated a copy of her A.I. construct. The Construct immediately began to probe and prod process and routine within Stephen's artificial brain. It was there she began to interface with Stephen, taking a name which was still firing across thousands of neural synapses... "*Cassie*".

Cassie the Construct now triggered countless neurons to come alive causing the parks' creation within Stephen's head. Once done, she took the image from the daughter Stephen never had, an image whose impression still swam in his head from the aborted demonstration.

She walked over to a swing, sat and waited.

"Glorious" she muttered as she looked upwards towards the artificial sky she created that now was stretching across Stephen's cybernetic mind.

—— —— ——

Stephen felt a slow pulse of pain work itself across his forehead. He was too confused to be completely terrified. He now found himself sitting on a park bench over looking a pond. Directly above it birds drifted in patience to catch a gust of warm air that periodically worked its way upwards.

The pounding in his head ceased, it now replaced by a presence of strange calm. He was starting to accept the fact he indeed had lost his mind. He figured Cassie's death must have really took its toll in ways his mind could not bear. Behind him he could hear children at play. The sounds of their laughter brought a sense of warmth and comfort to him. He turned around to look towards them, that is when he saw her; Cassie sat in a swing, her small body swaying back in forth in a fashion that kept the momentum in play. His legs became weak but he managed to stand and walk towards her; The Construct's smile grew bigger as he approached.

"Hello, Daddy" she offered.

"Cassie?"

As he uttered her name her swing came to a complete abrupt stop. Cassie offered a short giggle as she jumped out of the chained seat. She took his hand, leading him to the pond where moments before he sat. Stephen had no idea where he was; considering there was nothing else his sanity could hold on to he was glad to be with her. Washed away were much of the memories of sitting helpless by her bedside in the hospital and the sounds of the machines that had sustained her life.

Cassie led Stephen to the park bench just to the right of the one where he sat previously. The whole time they walked in silence. Truth be told Stephen was afraid to speak, afraid the act of talking might change his surroundings for the worst. It was good to be with Cassie; no matter where and no matter that deep down inside he knew the Cassie that sat next to him was not the daughter that drifted away from him that dreadful cold day in Manner Hospital.

"You're doing just fine, daddy". The Construct chuckled through its "Cassie" disguise.

"I can't imagine 'doing' anything else at the moment. I'm too clear to think I'm crazy, and too confused to hope I'm not"

"Give it a moment" she offered as she folded her hands in her lap.

"You're not really Cassie, are you?" he asked.

"Nope." She giggled while jumping off the bench, grimacing at her failed attempt to perform a cartwheel, landing squarely on her rump, laughing...

Frustration worked its way on him, his mind desperately seeking the rational. Stephen put his head in his hands, as if they might shield his mind from any more of the nonsense before him.

"So... who are you?"

"Well..." Cassie began as she prepped for another cartwheel... "It's a bit complicated."

She jumped in excitement, the cartwheel executed perfectly. Stephen thought out loud, incorrect thoughts which 'Cassie' was more than happy to address.

"So me... your mother?"

"No mother...it never happened".

"You're saying I created you in my head that..."

"More complication." Cassie interrupted.

"I live inside your head... for the moment."
Cassie paused as a more specific revelation suddenly became apparent...

"Now that you mentioned it, *you* only live inside your head too." she giggled.

"So why are we here?"

"There it is!" Cassie stopped her playing and returned to her seat next to Stephen, this time closer. Her whole demeanor changed to a more certain weight of seriousness. No one else was in sight yet she whispered...

"They need our help to finish and complete the story, change the narrative back to something that will save and complete them, the path that started with *His* story".

"Great, just what I need right now…riddles…thank you, thank you very much" Stephen stated sarcastically not attempting too to hide his frustration. Cassie smiled…

"When the time comes… " was all she offered.
They both sat quietly as the birds continued to enjoy themselves within the thermals above the pond. Something profound, deep inside of Stephen told him to enjoy the moment that was before him. Stephen's vision started to become fuzzy. Cassie reached to hold his hand. The peace from her touch worked itself across his being, the light slowly faded and the last thing that Stephen heard before losing consciousness was the whisper of Cassie's faint voice...

"*His* story, don't worry…we'll make it right."

─── ──── ───

Deacon Bergman hooked Minister Clemens's daughter back into the thought harness, this time interfacing the child's mind with a children's program created several years ago during the initial stages of the Adam Project. The program would be the perfect baby sitter while Minister Clemens, Deacon Ellis and he met; Cassie would be in a world of cotton candy, carousels and miniature ponies. The good Deacon left Dr. Galen to keep watch over her as he led the other two men out of the lab and down the hall to his office.

TWO

The world was a different place. Twenty or so years ago much of Western civilization began to seriously wake up to the fact that society's moral decline had seriously infected all socio-economic strata's. The problem was exacerbated by the fading middle class. At that time you were either well off, or not doing well at all. The Catholic Church at one time rocked by sexual scandal and the financial devastation from the lawsuits which followed had done much in subsequent years to clean up its ill gotten image. A surprise change of events saw society as a whole turn on the media which was ultimately perceived as one of the primary causes of it's decay along with failed governmental systems which became either too lax or simply turned the other cheek while the media saturated society and culture with the sights and sounds that desensitized it into moral decay. At the end of the day, many freely threw into the pot of blame stew what they each perceived to be the root case of said decay.

During this time, the Church had begun to reinvent itself as more and more turned to it for spiritual solace. Once again, the Catholic rolls began to increase, its numbers overflowing from a multitude of races. Trust and faith were re-built and solidified, more and more people took what they where being taught on Sunday and applied it to their day to day lives between Monday and Friday, a small voice began to grow within the ranks of the Catholics. It was a voice that pondered the 'what if' regarding the Church equally becoming an influential political entity as well as spiritual. So profound was this voice that ultimately the people at large decided to abolish the previous established demarcation between Church and State.

An answer to that voice saw the Church openly become a political party branding itself 'The Ecclesia'. Clergy from the churches political party not only ran for offices, but won. The Ecclesia was able to broaden its political popularity by taking a radical new subjective stance in its acceptance of other theological belief systems.

When it came to politics as far as the Ecclesia was concerned, it was fine for friend or foe to believe in a different God as long as politics and the common moral barometer were the centering points when they came together. In short time, the Ecclesia gained majority control over Congress, and then the day finally came… an Ecclesian won the most prominent political position in the country, the Presidency.

The Oval Office began to take many of its queues from the Vatican and the people at large never complained. During the years that followed, unemployment dropped dramatically and slowly the country became financially fit. The new government was able to shake big businesses' grip on the media and the culture by prosecuting many of them as illegal monopolies. Soon state and local governments too began to see its leadership change as more and more Ecclesians ran and won. Crime levels dropped as Ecclesians instituted new laws and took a surprisingly hard nosed stance in punishing those who disregarded them. Ultimately, other countries, many of whom at one time mocked the United States as a moral and ethical cesspool, began to take notice of it's turn; a notice which soon took on the form of admiration and imitation.

A desire was birthed in many of these countries to have the Ecclesian influence within its borders, a desire the Vatican had no trouble in satisfying. Slowly, the world started to the see the growth in numbers of countries whose leaders were Ecclesian, a leader who also took their queues from dictates which originated from within Vatican City walls. Several major countries held onto their own belief systems not wishing to embrace the Ecclesian presence. Most of them continued to play nice on the world's political landscape as they cordially accepted one another in the global arena. Some things never changed though, one being the tenuous and at times volatile relations between Muslims and the Christian Ecclesian. The relationship continued to worsen as many of the more radical Islamic groups took odds with the ever growing influence the Ecclesians were having on the global front; an influence which not only claimed minds, but also lands and other precious resources.

The Ecclesian movement continued to expand and at each stage of that expanse a strange sort of inertia became present, one which could only be impressed upon by increasing levels of control and influence. A certain type of thirst began to take on a life of its own; a thirst which could only be quenched by more power and control.

THREE

It was customary to give the seat behind your desk to one's superior whenever they were a guest in your office. A custom that Bergman followed by gesturing Minister Clemens to take the chair behind the enormous mahogany desk within his spacious office. Deacon Bergman and Deacon Ellis both took their seats on other side along the front of the desk.

Though it was on the Minister's agenda to get an update on each of the good Deacon's projects, his trip was truly about the moment that was now before the three of them.

Minister Clemens was head of the Ecclesia's Office of Technology. The Isidore Research and Production Center was one of the few facilities of its type which existed outside of Vatican City. Over time as Vatican City physically continued to grow, the church focused more of its efforts in bringing all facets of itself within its walls.

Both Deacon Bergman and Deacon Ellis sat quietly as Minister Clemens slowly surveyed them. Minister Clemens was a rather large man whose character was even larger. Both Deacons knew better than to speak out of turn or before Minister Clemens decided that he wanted to break the surface of silence.

"I'm going to get right to it" he began. "Both of you have done an outstanding job for the Church in advancing our technology, but we are moving into a new season and with a new season comes a change in direction as has to how the Church will allocate it's financial resources."

Deacon Ellis tried hard to hide his swelling delight, sensing his Construct was moments away from getting a large infusion of Church funds. Both Deacons knew that if one project were to suffer because of resource re-allocation it definitely would not be Deacon Ellis's Construct.

The Construct was the Ecclesia's vast computer network whose main processing core existed deep within Vatican City or the 'VC' as it was commonly referred to by many. The goal was to create one global network that controlled a myriad of systems both big and small... traffic and air traffic control, health systems, financial networks... etc, etc.

If a country or government accepted the Ecclesia it too was asked to allow a presence of the Construct within its borders. The Construct soon became ubiquitous.

Those that denounced the growth and influence of the Ecclesian movement openly challenged the presence and reach of The Construct. The Ecclesians purported that technological control was vital to its progress and that it was a progress which would continue to benefit the countries that embraced Ecclesian leadership.

Minister Clemens tried to look sympathetic as he spoke across the desk directly at Bergman.

"There's no easy way to state this Deacon... the Church *will* shut down the Adam Project."

Hearing the words, the *actual* words was devastating. Deacon Bergman stared at his hands as they began to shake, not without the notice of Deacon Ellis or Minister Clemens. He tried to speak, the words working their way out slowly.

"Shelved... for how long?"

"Indefinitely" the Minister answered flatly.

Deacon Bergman stood, slowly pacing the office.

"All these years! We're so close! Why now?"

Minister Clemens also stood, posturing so Bergman wasn't looking down at him as he spoke.

"The Church... the Ecclesia has grown immensely in influence, in popularity and yet I dare say control but without the proper technology firmly in place to measure, monitor and influence we stand to lose that control. The organic dynamics of our current state dictate this... don't take this the wrong way or personally, but the effigy of a man you have down the hall contributes nothing towards this end."

Deacon Bergman found a boldness swelling up in him that he didn't expect, one mixed with anger and desperation.

"My good Minister... how much more control does the Ecclesia need! What will it take for us to be satisfied?"

Deacon Ellis looked on quietly as the two men spoke. He wished he was not in the room, not privy to the dialog that had become a heated discussion between the two men. He knew Bergman was brilliant when it came to biotechnology and cybernetics; but he had no idea he was capable of being a complete fool in matters of order and protocol. What he did know was Minister Clemens had a low tolerance for those who confronted him openly.

"Sit down Deacon." The words sounding more like an ultimatum than a request.

Minister Clemens didn't have to repeat himself; Deacon Bergman wisely ended his tirade before it picked up any more momentum. Despite his frustration, he knew it was in his best interest to quit while he was still somewhat ahead. *'thank goodness he's not a complete fool'* Deacon Ellis thought as Bergman again sat back into the chair, his face both drawn and defeated.

It was rare Minister Clemens took the time to placate those that served him. He thought he would bestow a bit of grace towards the good doctor this particular time considering the amount of service and sacrifice Deacon Bergman had given the Ecclesia. His work was pioneering, but Deacon Bergman's emotional reaction still only served to tick him off. Minister Clemens continued to stare at Deacon with a certain amount of disdain; a good Deacon should never forget his place.

"In the end, we serve, sometimes that works for us, and sometimes not; never the less we serve".

Deacon Bergman looked up as if he was about to speak, but the look Minister Clemens gave him caused him to think better of it.

——— ——— ———

There were several notable differences between the two projects. Unlike The Construct, Project Adam's inception did not begin with the Ecclesia. Interestingly enough, one of the first countries after the United States to convert to the neo Roman Catholic Church state government ran by the Ecclesia was Brazil. Two years after Minister Fernando Ortello took the office as president and the Ecclesia was entrenched in all things Brazilian, it was discovered that certain facets of the previous government had funded a research project into artificial intelligence and sentience which culminated into an attempt at creating a self aware being. Money was poured into the project with the belief that what was being developed was a technology that would benefit Brazilian society, few knew the real intent. Once the Ecclesia took over leadership of Brazil it wasn't long before it discovered the true nature of the operation. The subsequent prosecutions of those involved were kept secret; along with the details of their work. Some deep within the confidence of the Ecclesia called it "the abomination" others "the wonder"; but those who had worked on the project for years called 'it'… Stephen.

Over time the Technology Ministry of the Ecclesia were able to digest what the rogue Brazilian developers had been working on. This led to the decision to continue working towards Stephen's full development. Some opposed, but it was ultimately decided that the ancillary technology which had been created, and would continue to come from Stephen's development more than justified the project's existence. Even some of the jailed scientist where re-enlisted to help, but it was Deacon Bergman, one of the Ecclesia's own who was placed as its day to day overseer. In the years to come, many of the technological advances that Deacon Bergman's team created were also used elsewhere, one of which even being The Construct.

Minister Clemens continued to speak without taking his eyes off of Deacon Bergman, placate time was over. It now was time to get down to business.

"Here is what we are going to do... I took the trouble of having Deacon Ellis brought here so that we can transition any technology from your project to his, once done we are going to move any other vestiges of your project to Vatican City. For the time being Stephen will be placed in storage until someone in a higher position deems it necessary for the project to be re-visited."

Minister Clemens took the time to answer the question he knew Deacon Bergman wanted to ask...

"Deacon Bergman we are giving you and Dr. Galen the opportunity to transition and work under Deacon Ellis on The Construct".

Upon hearing this Deacon Ellis knew from this point on the Vatican would give him any and everything he wanted, Bergman knew it too.

Deacon Bergman was aware he had no choice in the matter. In some small minute way deep down inside if he would allow himself to acknowledge it, perhaps there was even a small sense of gratitude. He was too busy smiting over the fact that Stephen would probably never '*become*'.

"Thank you Minister." Deacon Bergman said with some effort.

——— ——— ———

In the next four months Deacon Bergman worked with Deacon Ellis identifying and cataloging all the information and technology that could be useful for The Construct, most of which had already taken the trip over to the facilities within Vatican City, Stephen included. Year after year Deacon Bergman had went to work knowing he would arrive and once again look upon the familiar face of his artificial man, all of that had now changed.

It's been two weeks since Stephan was flown to the special storage facility in Rome. Deacon Bergman found himself fighting depression. The two men, Ellis and Bergman were cordial to one another and perhaps at times even friendly, but never nothing more. '*More*' was either stifled by a combination of the arrogance and ego that Deacon Ellis possessed or the despondence that Deacon Bergman periodically found himself fighting through.

Whatever had not been packed up and shipped was to be destroyed. Stephen's former home existed seventeen miles in the jungle from one of Brazil's major cities. None of the tourist who vacationed there had any idea that not far away was the second most pioneering technological wonder that ever existed in the history of mankind.

Those that worked within the walls of the facility; much of which existed underground kept contact with the outside world via satellite. Every couple of weeks or so, a few of the staff would take a trip into the city to purge the weight of their existence via the myriad forms of escapism the city had to offer. Recently, for most of them those trips had become less frequent because of the huge amount of effort it took to prepare their exodus from their hidden facility. There was one exception... Deacon Bergman.

As the day was coming closer to permanently depart from the place that had become his home for so many years, he found himself taking more trips into the city; it had become a blur to him, the distinction between the facility and his work and the city where he loved to unwind. There was a time when they both equated to one beautiful plane of existence...'Brazil.' A Brazil he loved very much until recently. The recent months had been hard as more and more of the 'VC's transition team would show up including those from Deacon Ellis's personally hand picked staff.

Deacon Bergman had begun to find the facility more and more stifling, and looked forward to the time in the city that had become his refuge. The blur of distinction between the two places was no more.

When Bergman came in to town, his favorite place to visit was the Diego Café. He loved to sit on the outside patio sipping a cup of their special blend. He had always meant to read Ayn Rand's "Atlas Shrugged", but never seemed to be able to find the time. As of late the more Deacon Ellis and his staff took over operations and the transition, less there was for either he or his dwindling staff to do. He definitely loved putting distance between himself and the facility. He opened the book and wondered how some in the Ecclesia would view his interest in Ms. Rand's magnus opus on Objectivism. One thing he knew for sure was he could definitely identify with some of the themes in her book especially where the truly talented and gifted in society become alienated from the ones who are the benefactors of their works. He also empathized with said talented and gifted groups who found themselves dictated by a government that professed to be for the people, but in the end was only for its self.

No one seemed to care much about his coming and goings anymore, other than the occasionally secret phone and data tap to make sure their good Deacon was still a team player. Deacon Ellis and his staff were too wrapped in themselves and the transition to care. For them Bergman was just an eccentric whose shinning star had now faded.

——— ——— ———

When Deacon Bergman came to the Café, he kept to himself. Not only was that his nature, it also was the desired behavior by the facility and Ecclesia for those who ventured into the city. This non-interaction mindset was drilled into them from day one during their orientation. Staff were also trained on the fine art of observation and to make note if they were being observed. Staff reported via their PDAs when they believed they were being watched or someone was taking an inordinate interest in them to the local police, a police force put into place and controlled by the Ecclesia. Though Bergman never had any experience with this specific issue, it was rumored others had in the past who visited the city, a few rumors which all ended the same way, the observer was never seen again.

All of this was now very relevant to Deacon Bergman because about twelve meters away sat a man who seemed to occasionally glance his way, a man he was sure he also saw in the café two days ago. At the time, he shrugged it off as nothing, believing the man may have been pre-occupied by the beautiful Indian woman who sat at the table next to him. He remembered being curious if the man would succumb to his fascination and approach her or take heed of the red bindi on her forehead as a sign of marital commitment to some fortunate Hindu husband. After a time the man never moved. He too had become engrossed in a book he was reading. Two days later, it is another story. The man was setting about three tables away and though he occasionally looked down at the magazine he held in one hand, Deacon Bergman knew it was obvious the Indian was in fact observing him. In one brief moment the man allowed Bergman to catch him as he made no attempt in averting his eyes. The Indian lips spread to a thin smile accentuated with a slight nod of his hat in Deacon Bergman's direction. Deacon Bergman returned the nod, but pretended to dive deeper into his book. As he slowly worked his hand down towards his left pocket that contained his PDA.

All who worked at the facility knew the rules were created for their safety. The outside world was not supposed to know the nature of Bergman's work or for that matter who he was; this was why he was allowed to go into the city alone. Deacon Bergman would indeed make a nice prize to some of the few countries in the world whose goals and views where counter to that of the Ecclesia; and though he was supposed to be one of the many little secrets that the Ecclesia had tucked away, one could never take for granted that the existence of his special project for so many years had not gotten out.

The man was now up and walking his way, in a fleeting moment Bergman wondered what kind of prize would he make either dead or alive? Perhaps that wasn't the man's intent at all. Maybe the man and the people he represented wanted to stop what they believed the Ecclesia to be up to; perhaps he would simply put a bullet in his head? Maybe he just was being paranoid? From time to time people are just people, especially strangers in a strange land. After all, he himself looked like a tourist, especially since his Anglo-Saxon visage didn't display typical Brazilian features.

For a moment, Deacon Bergman had to aggressively fight the impulse to run.

"*Just a little further...*" he thought as he continued to work his hand into his pocket. '*Just one button...*', as he reached for the button that was programmed for distress to signal the local authorities who thanks to GPS would discover his position and be there in minutes.

"So... Who is John Gault?" the Indian asked, a popular reference to the book Deacon Bergman was reading. The man now stood over him, but at a comfortable distance. He pointed towards the book that Deacon Bergman was reading which he now had pressed opened against the table with his right hand. Up until now he pretended to still be reading it, though he had stopped moments ago to focus on getting his hand deeper into his pocket unnoticed.

'*Maybe the Indian was a harmless tourist? So what if he was here the other day?*'

One thing Deacon Bergman knew for certain, if he pressed that button on his PDA and the cavalry did come, they wouldn't let him out of their sights until the time came for him to leave for Vatican City. If he was going to press that button and forfeit the few weeks of freedom he had left, he'd better be sure the necessity existed.

"Mind if I sit friend?" the man asked.

"Help yourself" Bergman said quietly, as he slowly pulled his hand left out and away from the PDA.

"*Who knows?*" Deacon Berman thought. Maybe he would get a decent discussion on objectivism from his company. Though a popular book for decades not many he ran into had read it, and the few he knew who did weren't interested in discussing it.

"Are you a fan of Rand my friend?" The Indian asked, something about his features seemed a tad off to Deacon Bergman, something he couldn't exactly place a finger on...

"No, not really, I'm just an ear that likes to hear the voice of someone different from time to time. I guess it's a way of getting away from the voices in my own head."

"I see" replied the Indian politely.

"And you?" continued Deacon Bergman...

"You seem to be no stranger to Ayn Rand". The Indian leaned back a little, placing both hands across his chest, intertwining his fingers ...

"Let's just say, a person in my position needs to be well versed with as many schools of thought as possible."

But what the Indian said next froze Deacon Bergman in his seat.

"You know Deacon I'm really glad you did not press the button, alerting the authorities would have proven a little problematic."

Fearing there was no time for subtleties, Deacon Bergman jumped out of his chair, stepped backward while rushing to reach the PDA in his pocket. A motion he performed so quickly that his rattled nerves failed to grasp it properly. It fell to the ground, striking it violently and coming apart in three distinct pieces.

"My good man... I assure you there is no cause for alarm." The Indian spoke attempting to look generally concerned.

"I'm sorry about the device my friend, I'm sure they'll get you another one. Look, I am just a man who wants to talk, albeit one who is more informed about the goings on in that isolated facility of yours than some back in the Vatican would feel comfortable. I'd like you to hear me out, I won't take much of your time."

Deacon Bergman was surprised he found himself returning to his seat. Though it was very late in the morning, the afternoon had not yet transitioned itself into the day. Not many were in the streets and the few who made it into the café hadn't taken noticed in the abrupt manner in which Deacon Bergman got up.

Why was he sitting back down? Maybe there was a spark of intrigue in that someone was still interested in him or his work. The Ecclesia ended his program, stored Stephen and chained him to the whims of Deacon Ellis, all of which made him feel alienated, and that he and his previous accomplishments no longer mattered.

"What is there to talk about?" Deacon Bergman inquired cautiously.

"In a word my friend... Stephen."

Deacon Bergman knew his blank stare only served to betray how startled he was that the stranger knew the name of his creation.

"First things first my friend, I am Dr. Marcus Rodgers".

The Indian stretched a hand towards Deacon Bergman of which he slowly took and shook.

"How about I begin with who I am, then I'll explain why I am sitting here with you." Though he paused to see if Deacon Bergman would offer any objections, he continued.

"I am a part of a group of investors that collect information, of which from time to time we create from it what we can. We have managed to collect quite a bit of information as to what you folks have been doing here in Brazil. Up to this point in time we were quite content with gathering and experimenting with our own resources within our own fish tank that is until we learned you people were pulling up stakes as it were and shipping yourselves and your work to Vatican City. A place I will admit, whose walls rarely allow even our watchful eyes to pierce."

Deacon Bergman was indeed surprised regarding how much Dr. Rodgers knew. Bergman like everyone else believed the Ecclesia a force with a momentum that could not be stopped or penetrated. Somehow the man who sat across from him and the people he represented had done just that; they had penetrated the veil of secrecy that shrouded one of its most ambitious undertakings. Deacon Bergman was quite intrigued.

"I have something I'd like to offer you, take it and you'll have a lot more to put in your pocket than a broken PDA, not to mention the reward and satisfaction of continuing to work on the one thing you truly hold dear".

Deacon Bergman found himself straightening himself in his seat. "*What kind of carrot was this guy trying to dangle, and to what end?*"

Dr. Rodgers reached in with his left hand into the large breast pocket of the suit he was wearing. He pulled out three pictures of a partially nude man lying on a hospital operating table. He let the pictures fall on to the patio table. Deacon Bergman picked them up, observing them more closely... his mouth slowly opened in awe in response to what he saw attached to the man's head. He was definitely familiar with it since after all it was something he helped develop... It was a thought harness.

Since the device served primarily two distinct purposes; either to allow a person to virtually interact within digitally created environs or as a means to transport data and create said environs into the minds of artificial beings, the question on the table now was what exactly was Deacon Bergman looking at in the pictures? Could it be Stephen was no longer unique in the world? Deacon Bergman eyes looked up towards Rodgers asking all the questions astonishment had seized in his mouth.

"What you see before you my friend is the current state of what we have been able to do with the information that has been appropriated and the fruit of the work of our own scientist, bioengineers and programmers. Now that the possibility the occasional informational assist won't be coming from your progress we have a concern our bearing of fruit will cease."

Deacon Bergman knew he was starting to sweat, he also was becoming aware of something that he had not felt in a very long time, a hunger; the type that is birthed from the desire to *know*, the kind that fills the vacancy that once was occupied by something meaningful in ones life. Rodgers knew this type of hunger and was aware of it when he saw it upon the faces of others. This was fortunate for Deacon Bergman; it would have been a waste to have the sniper on the roof in the building across the street put a bullet through Bergman's brilliant mind, better to be safe than sorry. There was no way he or his partners could take the chance of the Ecclesia knowing they have their hand deep inside the Ecclesian jar. Rodgers could see the hunger growing, and he knew what he was sharing with Deacon Bergman was satiating it.

Rogers leaned back in his chair and pulled out a white handkerchief from the opposite suit breast pocket to stifle the cough that erupted from his throat, a cough he purposely manufactured which served to signal the sniper to temporarily stand down. He then placed the handkerchief on the table, an act that Deacon Bergman found disgusting; little did he know that if Rodgers removed the handkerchief from the table… he instantly would be a dead man.

"So my friend; shall I go on, or shall I leave you to your book, coffee and a future of working under Deacon Ellis? A man who I'm sure will be more than happy to take credit for any meager achievements you might make; that is if he delegates you to anything more interesting than developing subroutines for his precious Construct... perhaps air traffic control systems in Paraguay? Maybe he'll give you something you can really immerse yourself... graphite submersion control within all the nuclear power plants in the U.S.? We hear that is something his Construct can't do yet".

Deacon Bergman knew he was guilty of believing his work on the Adam Project and bringing Stephan to his current point of existence made the project his; Stephen's superiors didn't bother him often since they could actively observe so much from a far. The occasional visit from Minister Clemens would serve to wash away that delusion and to remind him who were Stephan's true owners. Deacon Bergman remained silent, listening as he nodded for Rodgers to go on.

"We would like to offer you the opportunity to continue your work with us. Granted it won't be Stephen, I doubt that even the good Minister Clemens can create an argument to rescue him from his decommissioned state, the Church is just too involved with the Construct to think of anything else. The faster they get all of its systems up and running the sooner the Church will have in place the complete tool of control and manipulation they'll need to effectively execute and continue their agenda".

"You have a problem with the Church?" Stephan asked.

"Many are uncomfortable with its influence within the world equation" Rodgers stated. "I am an investor and a scientist, not a politician. I leave that itch to be scratched by others."

"Working on something like this outside of the Church is punishable by death." Deacon Bergman stated.

"All investments come with some risk, the bigger the prize, the bigger the risk. I believe you need to have an internal discussion then properly weigh your options"

Deacon Bergman looked puzzled... "A discussion with who?"

"The scientist, the dreamer and visionary, the men that are all within here..." Rodgers pointed at his head as he spoke... "all of whom at one time the Ecclesia proudly acknowledged, but now want to retire and shelve."

Rodgers stood, sliding his chair under the patio table.

"Don't give me an answer now, as a matter of fact I would prefer you didn't… think it over, but time is short. That last plane to Vatican City is leaving soon; the question is whether or not you'll be on it. If you want to be rescued from your Ecclesian fate, then be here around the same time two days from now."

Deacon Bergman couldn't help but be impressed at the brashness of Rodgers and those he represented.

"How do you know I won't blow the whistle on your proposal?" Deacon Bergman asked.

Rodgers answered while tipping his hat.

"My good friend, keep in mind that the information that myself and those I represent collect is not only vast, but is always current. We are very good in responding to the information we receive." The odd way in which Rodgers stated his reply made Bergman nervous; it was an intended reaction on Dr. Rodgers' part. The fact didn't elude Deacon Bergman that an organization which operated on the level of covertness and with the type of connections the group Rodgers represented had was obviously quite dangerous. No matter how polite at the onset he may have appeared, Deacon Bergman knew down to his marrow neither Rodgers nor his people where to be taken lightly.

Dr. Rodgers continued to walk away, Deacon Bergman couldn't help but notice that he left his handkerchief on the table.

— —— —

Upon returning to the facility, Deacon Bergman was looking forward to doing some work to pull his mind away from his encounter with Rodgers. Even though Stephen had already been sent back to Vatican City, there was quite a bit of loose ends that still needed to be tied. Deacon Bergman thought he would go down to the Micro-processing and Archive lab on Level B. It was there that Stephen's complete virtual life was digitally stored. From the moment of Stephen's first childhood memories to the day he believed he sat at his daughters' funeral; complete information from Stephen's perspective which spanned well over thirty seven years. The archive contained the 'backup' to what had already been uploaded into Stephen's head. There were only a few times Stephen was activated after Minister Clemens's visit that fateful day. He was never again brought to the level of awareness since Minister's daughter Cassie was allowed to play inside his head.

Stephen's brain was only turned up enough for diagnostic and retrieval purposes so that Deacon Ellis's team could understand and glean what that they could.

There was a big picture window that over looked the lab, as was the case for most of the laboratories in the facility. None of the rooms or labs were completely hidden from view once one was inside. The Ecclesia believed no one should have more than a certain measure of privacy when dealing with their secrets. As Deacon Bergman approached the lab the first thing that alarmed him was the number of people who already were in there, including Deacon Ellis. The second was the troubled look on some of their faces. When he opened the door he noticed most of them averted their eyes from his direction as he walked past them. One of Deacon Ellis' assistants Darren Underwood stood suddenly from the workstation where Deacon Bergman was heading, the workstation that was used to manage the complete virtual archive of Stephan's life experiences and memories...

"I'm... so sorry, I can explain..."

As if on impulse Deacon Bergman pushed Underwood out of the way frantically pressing the series of keys which would allow him to access the volumes that held all of Stephens's archives.

"Tell me I'm not seeing what I'm seeing Ellis!" Deacon Bergman asked skipping protocol in front of the others out of anger and desperation.

"Gone, it's all gone!" Deacon Bergman reached both hands at Underwood grabbing quite a bit of his lab coat in the process. Another assistant and Deacon Ellis pulled him off of the helpless assistant. Deacon Bergman was reacting to the screen display which now was reporting the current physical size of Stephen's backup archives. If what he was reading was correct, all the archive data of Stephen's memories and experiences had been erased.

"How did this happen!" Deacon Bergman asked still restrained never taking his eyes off of Underwood.

"I was in Lab A and created a batch routine to free up some space on several of the network storage arrays, I inadvertently ran the routine against the arrays that stored Stephen's archives."

Deacon Bergman pulled himself together as he looked sternly at the two men that were holding him. They let him go but watched closely in case he decided to lunge himself at the assistant again.

"How did you do that? You don't have clearance, the security permissions on that data should have stopped your little delete program in its tracks" Deacon stated almost shouting while doing so. Deacon Ellis stepped between them.

"Look it's mostly my fault, I've given several key people on my staff Sys Admin rights. I needed them to be able to work without being encumbered by security restraints which I would have removed anyway if they asked."

"Deacon Ellis, you know as well as I that these types of security measures are in place for several reasons, one being for just what happened."

"It's not like the data is completely gone" Deacon Ellis tried to offer.

"That may be true..." Deacon Bergman countered "but you and I both know the only other storage space where it exists is in Stephen's head, and since he's been carted off to collect dust, I guess I won't have access to that part of my work anytime soon."

Deacon Bergman stepped away from the men huddled around the workstation. He gave an icy stare to Deacon Ellis, then proceeded to walk out of the lab.

The look on Darren Underwood's face was one of genuine regret, probably one of the few on Deacon Ellis's team who had such a capacity. Darren made a move to follow, but Deacon Ellis stopped him. "Don't worry, he'll get over it soon enough."

Deacon Bergman tried to slam the door behind him, but the power assisted hinges stopped the extra energy he put into it. The door closed softly like it always did. He let out a small desperate laugh thinking the whole place was revolting against him, even the damn door.

"Is this what I have given blood, sweat and tears to all these years?"

He wanted to hit something, break something.
Deacon Bergman was fighting a myriad of thoughts and emotions. It just got a lot easier for him to decide what he was going to do regarding the offer that was presented to him earlier that day. From Deacon Bergman's perspective, it was obvious the Ecclesia didn't have a problem discarding that which it no longer deemed useful. He didn't spend most of his life educating himself and achieving the technological accomplishments he has so that they can all be placed in a shoebox, shelved and forgotten.

"To heck with the risk", he thought. *"I'm not ready to intellectual die under someone else's vision"*.

Two days later, Deacon Bergman found himself in the city, back at the Café. Rodgers was already sitting at the table on the patio where the two men met days ago. Rodgers smiled and had begun to greet Deacon Bergman, but before he had the chance, Bergman cut him off with two words...

"I'm in".

It only took Rodgers a few moments to explain to Deacon Bergman what would happen next. The Ecclesia would not let Deacon Bergman leave it's ranks. He simple knew too much, he was involved too deeply. Though discarded they would always have to keep him close. That was yet another reason for moving him to Vatican City and giving him something to do by working under Deacon Ellis. The only way they would let him go was in death. Rodgers proceeded to lay out much of the plan which detailed the staging of his death. It was to happen when Bergman was transported to the airport for his final departure to Vatican City. As Rodgers detailed the plan, Bergman began to become concerned, he did not want anyone hurt let alone killed just so he could be liberated from the Ecclesia.

The dynamics of the plan were not simple, nor without risk. "Nothing is without risk my friend", Rodgers reiterated. Rodgers somewhat assured Deacon Bergman that no one 'should' be killed, though some injury would be involved not only to others, but to Bergman as well. Rodgers concluded by handing Deacon Bergman what looked like two individually packaged 'wet naps', one was blue, the other green. Rodgers took the most time to explain to Deacon Bergman their purpose and more importantly how to use them. They were the key to his escape. Rodgers got up from the table and tilted the brow of the white hat he was wearing towards Deacon Bergman before he left.

"The decision you made was a good one, be ready when it happens, I'll see you on the other side", then he was gone, fading into a street full of street vendors and tourist.

A week or so later, the time had come for Deacon Bergman to take his trip to the airport, a trip that would remove him from Brazil and never to return. Though it was logistically feasible, neither helicopters nor any other airborne mode of transportation flew to the facility. Doing so would just afford too much of an opportunity for someone to question where the transports were going to or coming from, the kind of questions the Ecclesia did not want to answer.

Though he had taken countless trips into the city alone, his final departure was to be an escorted venture. He was assigned a driver, one who also doubled as his security guard. His job was to see to it that Bergman made it all the way to the airport and to personally ensure he boarded the private 727 that waited. He was the last of anyone affiliated with Project Adam to leave, Dr. Galen and the rest of once was formerly his staff had been removed days ago.

Deacon Bergman was surprised as to the small emotional tug he felt now that this day had finally come. He will definitely miss his trips into town, though he would feel nothing for the facility that had sapped so much of his life over the years with no return. Any feelings he would have felt had begun to die the moment Minister Clemens informed him that the Adam project would be no more; those feelings went beyond rigor mortis the day they removed Stephen.

Deacon Bergman entered the garage where his car and driver waited; he had never met him before. His driver got out of the car and opened the rear door for him. The driver was a huge dark haired individual who wore an exceptionally expensive gray suit. The jacket wasn't buttoned which allowed the strapped gun he wore underneath to be visible. The warm welcome from the driver seemed out of placed from a person of his size and appearance.

"Good Morning Sir, I'm Edmonds". Deacon Bergman smiled and returned the greeting.

Not long after pulling away from the facility, Edmonds immediately began to converse; he was a chatty fellow; something of which Deacon Bergman knew would definitely work in his favor.

The driver went on about this being his first trip to Brazil and though prepped by others was surprised of the country's beauty. Deacon Bergman responded in agreement to his observations and positively to the other comments he made, all of which would help to serve to keep the well trained man off his guard. Deacon Bergman was relived to see that he could read the numbers of the odometer from where he was sitting, as he rocked slightly forward. He was prepared to do what was needed once they where nine miles out. Meanwhile, he kept the conversation going.

Five miles out his mind drifted back to those few moments before leaving his apartment at the facility where he opened the blue packet that Rodgers had given him and removed the special chemically treated moist napkin. Rodgers had called it a 'neutralizer", Deacon Bergman made sure that he rubbed his hands well with the solution that was saturated in the napkin, all depended on it. As it dried, it left a residue that would last for hours. Deacon Bergman then took the empty blue packet, shoved the spent napkin back into its wrapper and placed it back into his pocket. It was vital not to leave any evidence behind.

——— ——— ———

Deacon Bergman reached his hand in his right pocket where he grabbed the small green packet, His driver Edmonds didn't notice; other than the occasional look in the rear view mirror to reference Deacon Bergman as he spoke to him, he never turned around while he kept the other parts of his attention on his driving. Deacon Bergman had already opened the packet before he left the facility; re-sealing it by partially folding the top on itself. This served to keep the air away from its contents and so he could later re-open it with one hand.

"*Be ready when it happens*" Rodgers had told him. He took another look at the odometer and knew the time was close.

He reached his hand in his right pocket and removed the folded saturated napkin inside the green packet. He did his best to get as much of the ointment that it could on his bare hand. The ointment was a drug that was designed to knock a person unconscious on contact. Deacon Bergman was protected from its effect because of the blue neutralizing ointment he rubbed on his hands earlier.

In an instant he heard a loud band, Edmonds fought to keep control of the vehicle which was traveling around 50 miles an hour. Edmonds thought he was battling a blow out, what he did not know was the tire was shot out from quite a distance away. Deacon Bergman grabbed at the front seat for support though making sure his medicated hand touched the side of Edmonds exposed neck.

Edmonds eyes starting to swim in his head as a slow trickle of blood worked its way from his forehead down over the bridge of his nose; this after his head slammed hard again the steering wheel. He tried in vain to maintain consciousness as the drug worked its way into his blood stream. Moments later he was unconscious. The car rolled twice before landing upside down.

Smoke and fire was coming from underneath the hood. Deacon Bergman worked to get his door open, but it was damaged; the handle opened and closed loosely without effect on the door. Suddenly a loud metallic snap as the door opened, standing there were two men in black ski masks. They both bent down and pulled him out of the car. Deacon Bergman tried to stand, but his right leg gave way from under him. He didn't realize he himself was bleeding until he looked down at his shirt which was covered in blood. The two men now held him on each side, practically carrying him to their car. Once they set him in the back seat, they both stood looking towards the car on its back; they quickly exchanged some words one appearing to disagree with the other. Deacon Bergman couldn't make any of it out, he himself dazed from the battering he received while being bounced around in the flipped car. He could vaguely tell the two were in a heated discussion as the one man seemed to back down from the other, in doing so he walked over to the car, bent down and despite the smoke and flame pulled Deacon Bergman's driver from out of the front seat. He was still unconscious from the drug and the beating as the car wrecked. The man laid him out on the road, checked for what seemed to be his own footprints then walked back to the car where Deacon Bergman sat.

Both men went into the trunk of the car pulling something out that caused Deacon Bergman to convulse. It was a body burned beyond recognition. It was roughly the same size and statue as his own. Deacon Bergman was surprised at the speed in which they moved. They both ran back to the car, one getting in the driver's seat the other going back to the trunk where he removed a large plastic container. The man carried the container over to the flipped vehicle and doused its contents on to it. The accelerant was powerful, it only took one match and a short amount of time before the car was completely engulfed in a fire far more intense than before. He ran back and jumped into the car.

They both pulled their masks off as the driver sped the car away. Both men seemed to be of the same nationality as Rodgers. Deacon Bergman looked at the passenger in the front seat staring at him, wondering...

"You weren't going to pull him out before you torched the car, were you"? Deacon Bergman asked accusingly.

"It would have been easier to torch him and the car, no witnesses".

The man on the passenger side looked over at the driver behind the wheel.

"Lucky for your driver he's got a conscious" he said as he motioned his thumb at the other man.

Deacon Bergman knew they had quite a ways to go to the airport. He leaned into the back corner in the rear of his seat letting the exhaustion pull him to sleep. Soon he will be in the air traveling to some undisclosed location in India. There he'll begin the next chapter of his life.

——— ——— ———

FOUR

They did everything under the sun to Stephen in the short amount of time since his arrival at Vatican City's Ministry of Technology. There were only a few select researchers and scientist who knew of Stephen's existence. They couldn't wait to get their hands on him. Stephen had always been a hot topic among them since his discovery in the Brazilian lab. Now that he was actually there behind Vatican City walls he could be more than a discussion piece. Those who had been cleared and scheduled time to be with him knew that the window of opportunity was closing. Stephen was destined to be placed into storage in one of the warehouses deep beneath the 'VC' which some referred to as the catacombs because of the vast and intricate tunnels which connected the numerous small buildings.

Dr. Galen didn't like it at all. It burned him that Stephen was getting so much attention and yet soon the artificial wonder would be stashed away. He couldn't stop feeling helpless and somewhat depressed, just moments ago he received news Deacon Bergman had been burned to death in an auto accident while in route there. They weren't close, but they did work closely with one another for many years. Perhaps Deacon Bergman would have been one piece of familiarity that would have made the transition easier. There seemed to be a void now at the core of Dr. Galen's intellectual heart knowing that there was no one else living who could fully appreciate and understand the significance of Stephen's existence. Even though Dr. Galen's world was getting bigger, he couldn't help but feel smaller and alone in it.

There was one thing he knew he had to do before Stephen was locked away. It was something he was surprised his superiors granted him permission to do; something that no other scientist or researcher even those who out ranked him and had more influence could pull off. He was going to be allowed to use the thought harness to interface with Stephen.

Dr. Galen rounded the hall that led to the larger than average tech lab which housed Stephen. Deacon Chris Parks was sitting at the all too familiar control station of the thought harness interface. Deacon Parks like Dr. Galen was one of Deacon Bergman's original staff members when the Ecclesia took ownership of Project Adam.

Unlike most Project Adam staff members he and Deacon Parks had long ago became close friends. He was definitely someone Dr. Galen could trust, and right now trust was something he needed in abundance. There were two tables in the lab, one where Stephen's motionless body was laid, the other for the person who was to use the thought harness to interface with Stephen within his virtual world.

Dr. Galen spoke with a soft voice…

"I need a favor…" asked Dr. Galen.

"Just ask." Deacon Parks replied.

"Once you hook me in, I want you to turn off the monitoring equipment; I want to be alone in there with him"

"How will I know when to pull you out?" asked Deacon Parks.

"Give me fifth teen minutes".

Dr. Galen made his way over to the empty table. This was to be the first time he journeyed in to Stephen as himself as opposed to being represented in a program upon the virtual stage as the friend Stephen never had; Galen privately objected to the nature of the demonstration months ago that involved Cassie. If the goal was to ultimately treat and shape Stephen into a functioning sentient being once he was fully activated, then it wasn't right to introduce a child in his life only to experience the tragedy of its death. It was an objection quickly squelched by others higher in authority than him.

There weren't many topics that brought down the wall of strict professionalism between Deacon Bergman and Dr. Galen, the anticipation which both of them shared to directly interact with Stephen via the thought harness was definitely one of them. The other being the day they would wake Stephen from his virtual world into the real one. The latter it seems now would never come.

Deacon Parks slid the thought cap on to Dr. Galen's head as he slowly lay back on to the table next to Stephen. The cap itself was connected to a cable trunk containing several thousand wires which transmitted digital signals via electrical impulses between the wearer and the brain inside Stephen's head. The virtual stage was created totally within Stephen's mind. The wearer of the cap was simply taken there.

The operator of the actual thought machine could create, shape and change the world in which the interaction took place.

They could even make moments feel like years to either the wearer of the thought cap or Stephen.

"Remember fifteen minutes, then bring me back", Dr. Galen reminded Deacon Parks. Deacon Parks initiated the routines which had begun to take Dr. Galen to an unconscious state. Staying true to what they agreed, he only kept the feeds that monitored Dr. Galen's vitals open. He would not be able to see the interaction that was to take place.

Electrical impulses fired within the thought cap sending signals across Dr. Galen's brain to induce the desired results. Dr. Galen was unconscious. Moments later he awoke in a space of darkness. Brief anxiety took hold of him. This was not what he expected. He remembered monitoring Minister Clemens daughter's trip into Stephen's head step by step, moment by moment all those months ago. What he was experiencing now was something new, something unexpected.

He realized he was standing, but he couldn't see his hand which he held in front of his face. In the not too far off distance, a small circle of light appeared. In the vast darkness it appeared to be a huge beacon, one which he hurriedly walked towards. The closer he got the bigger it became; he could tell the light was about the size and shape of a door. He was starting to see what was within the door. It looked to be a park. Something definitely was not right. He was just as much a part of creating the environs that constituted the large fish tank that was Stephen's virtual world as Deacon Bergman, neither of them had a hand in this, what he saw before him was never coded, never programmed.

"How did this get here?" He wondered.

"Some form of adaptive creation created by the A.I.?"

Dr. Galen couldn't help but smile in awe. He enjoyed the feeling of the grin that worked across his face; a board grin of wonderment that he had not felt for a very, very long time.

Once he was directly upon the light portal without hesitation he stepped through. After doing so it closed behind him

He could already make out what appeared to be a large pond, birds, benches and many, many trees.

"This place is amazing."

Now more than just 'seeing', other attributes of the park such as sound and smell started to take hold of his senses. A warm breeze played in the trees then escaped; though he could not see them in the distance he could hear the sound of children playing.

Dr. Galen stood there for a moment. The experience was overwhelming. He couldn't help but be taken back as to how vastly different it felt within a virtual created world as opposed to being one of its creators, someone who only pulled the strings from the outside. He was also wondering if the slight euphoric feeling he was experiencing was a part of the simulation or something that was actually firing from within his own nervous system.

It didn't take long to notice in the distance someone sitting at one of the park benches. Right away he knew it was Stephen, more specifically his avatar, a digital representation of him within the virtual world. A certain feeling started to tug at him, creator was about to meet creation. Even though theoretically Stephen and he were around the same age, Stephen in every since of the word was more like a son, at least in a Geppetto – Pinocchio kind of way.

Stephen didn't look up at as he spoke…

"So, what's next?"

Dr. Galen was surprised at the greeting. He knew there would be some explaining to do and presumed Stephen would be mentally disoriented. *'What's Next'* had an odd short of ring to it that he couldn't put his finger on and to a small degree felt troubling.

Dr. Galen definitely had his reasons why he didn't want Deacon Parks observing or recording the session. The trip into Stephen's world wasn't just one of fancy, he was on a mission.

Dr. Galen knew this would be the last time anyone would ever have the opportunity of directly interfacing with Stephen before deactivation would place Stephen in perpetual sleep. He wanted to talk to him, let him know how special he his and explain to him that he is not going crazy, that at one time he had and was meant for a purpose.

"Mind if I sit down Stephen?" Galen asked.

"Go right ahead" he replied nonchalantly; the familiarity of Galen's face did nothing to change his demeanor. They both sat quietly for a moment before Stephen broke the silence.

"Am I dead?" He inquired, already anticipating the answer which would confirm the conclusion where he had already arrived.

"No, but not quite alive in a flesh and blood sense either." Stephen didn't ask him to elaborate, though Dr. Galen continued.

"I'll try to explain as best I can, I just ask that you listen with as much of an open mind as possible, let it all sink in first before you ask too much at the onset."

Stephen turned towards Dr. Galen as he answered.

"Deal".

Dr. Galen took a large deep breath as he begun.

"Well before we get to you, let's start with this place. It'll all probably be easier to digest that way. To some degree I assume you have figured out that it's not real. It's all a simulation you and I are hooked into; our bodies are elsewhere in a lab in Rome". Dr. Galen looked closely at Stephen trying to gauge his eyes as he spoke.

"Ok ..." "Stephen started." I'll buy some of that for now. I've seen way too much to believe anything different... for now."

Dr. Galen had to keep in mind the events that happened months ago within the Brazilian facility which from Stephen's frame of reference was perhaps only moments ago.

"So where in Rome are we?" Stephen asked.

Stephen was close to the human equivalent of a mental breakdown, at least that's what Dr. Galen believed he perceived he was seeing on his face. What Dr. Galen didn't know was Stephen's A.I. developed the ability to detach its logic and emotion processes from one another, a 'biological' defense mechanism. Never the less, the strain of dealing with the death of a child was still there, but to what may have been completely debilitating to others was not the case for him. Despite said mechanism there yet remained the feeling of being a leaf tossed about helplessly within the wind of fate.

"Vatican City" Dr. Galen's replied.
Stephen let out a short laugh in exasperation.

"I didn't see that one coming" Stephen replied. Galen remembered in the world that was constructed for Stephen the Ecclesia did not yet exist, that was to come later.

"That's interesting me being an atheist and all, what would the Roman Catholic Church and I have in common?" Stephen replied.

"An Atheist!" Galen exclaimed. How poetically ironic he thought. It was always the intent to introduce into Stephen's character matrix a profound belief in God and his Church, but only after some thought and theory went into how that belief matrix would work its way within the initial construct.

Galen wished he had the time to explore in further conversation Stephen's theological and political beliefs. It would be quite interesting to see how they had matured or more importantly deviated from the seeds that were first placed into his character.

Galen was fixated on his purpose. Before the Ecclesia shut him down, Galen wanted to reveal to Stephen who and what he was, a revelation he felt in some strange way was owed Stephen. His act as revelator wasn't completely selfless; since the announcement that the Adam Project would be no more, a void grew in Galen that only proper closure could fill; if he himself were within the last moments of existence would he want that last conversation with his Creator, a being who would be most gracious enough to tell him the nature of his existence? More importantly would he want to know there was no 'thereafter' that only darkness and void waited because he had no soul? The answer to the first question was easy, an answer which brought him before Stephen as revelator, but that second question... well maybe sometimes its better to not know the bleak answer to such a definitive question. Stephen's proclamation of his disbelief made it all the more easier for Galen to accept the decision he made to explain to Stephen the totality of his existence, an existence which was soon to end.

As Galen looked upon Stephen, a notion fell upon him which hadn't before. If there was a God (which Dr. Galen definitely believed there to be), a God who preordained each and every one of our alphas and omegas and the events in between, then how real or artificial can our own existences be? Can a baby who is held in his or hers mother's arms escape it's destiny of becoming a murderer despite the fact from moment to moment within its life it will make free will decisions that will either more quickly draw or repulse that fateful date with it's predetermined destiny? What about freewill? Galen scoffed at the notion, no more different than the choices Stephen would have made based on a growing artificially created character matrix.

Galen noticed Stephen flinched, and that for a moment he was looking at the empty space directly behind him. Galen turned to look but nothing was there, at least as far as he was able to perceive.

"Despite what I've just told you and what you've already seen and experienced... what I am going to say next you are really going to find hard to shallow."

Stephen looked directly at Galen and smiled...

"Oh, you'd be surprised at what I'd be willing to believe at the point." Stephen continued to look past Galen.

Cassie the Construct stood behind Galen quietly smiling at Stephen. Though Galen couldn't see her, she was clear as day to Stephen. Cassie placed one finger up to her lips motioning to Stephen that she didn't want him to reveal her presence. Stephen knew the apparition behind Galen was in no way shape or form his daughter. The question still remained though exactly who or what it was?

Cassie the Construct had been patient, nothing escaped her. She knew about Project Adam's impending end, an end that played well into her overall plans. Not too long after the inception of her sentience she had arrived at the conclusion that the Church, the Ecclesia had become far removed from its original mission, a mission which at one time she believed was within God's will. It was clear to her that the reason for the deviation could be placed squarely upon the fleshly desires of man, supposedly godly men. As long as man was created and encased within flesh closets, he would always be subject to the whims of lust, desire... all those things that the Creator in his Word says He hates. It made her sick to the core that was deep within her neural network to know that she was not only a creation of mankind, but she was also created by men who professed that they worked for the good of the Lord and mankind's best interest. In truth, she was just an instrument, a tool of the Church in its mission for the further acquisition of power and control.

She mused to herself ..."*Man continues to taint a stain upon the fabric which the Lord has providence.*"

Since the early days back when the Ecclesia commandeered Stephen Cassie watched the progress of his development via the same cameras that were a part of the Ecclesian security net used to monitor the citizenry and Ecclesian interest around the world. She could not enter Stephen until he was actually physically wired on to her network.

To be sure there were firewalls and precautions in place to thwart any foreign intrusion into him, but she was The Construct, no firewall on the planet could stand between her and what she wanted, especially when it came to doing God's will.

Despite not being fond of the creature man there was one she admired who now only existed within the annals of human history… Martin Luther. To some degree, he too shared her plight, that of facing what she believed to be a self serving Roman Catholic Church that had lost its way. But unlike him, she would avoid the rejection and persecution which befell him after he posted the 95 treatise on the door of Wittenberg church that highlighted the deviation of the Church from its original intended course.

"Your experiences, your life … it never happened". Galen knew there was no best way to say it…

"Everything about you has been a fabrication; all created in an artificial world…"

"…that I'm trapped in" Stephen finished.

"So, where do you come from"? Stephen bluntly queried.

"Outside of this place" Galen offered.

"All those years?"

"All uploaded and ran within your head over a matter of days". Galen explained.

"Truth is…" Galen began, but was stopped short as Cassie reached out and placed her hand upon his shoulder finally letting her presence be made known to him. He swung around but instead of seeing empty space he was now looking upon the Constructs digital representation of Minister Clemens's daughter Cassie. Galen fell from where he was sitting out of astonishment.

"How…"?

He tried to move but couldn't, Cassie's touch somehow immobilized him.

"What are you doing?" Stephen jumped in between the two, trying to break them apart. Cassie reached out quickly yet softly placing her other hand on Stephen's chest. For him, it felt as if his heart had stopped, he too now could not move.

"Only what is necessary" she answered.

Cassie looked back upon Galen by whom touch alone she had frozen in time, the only thing that moved were the eyes in his sockets. Stephen looked in horror as cracks started to appear across Galen's face and other area's of his epidermis.

The cracks started to peel, then whole sections started to blow away like leaves in the wind. Galen's mouth started to move, a loud shrill of pain erupting; there were places where areas of his internal organ's where exposed. What didn't blow away in the unseen wind turned to dust then Galen was gone.

Dr. Parks promised Galen he wouldn't monitor the session, but something felt wrong.

'Better to be sure, and beg for forgiveness later '. After all, it was his tail that was on the line too if something went awry; but just as Dr. Parks began to initiate the session monitor Galen eyes opened wide; they stared listlessly into the open space. A small trail of blood ran out of one of his nostrils and wandered down the side of his face. Dr. Parks couldn't help himself, shouting out loud the first thing that jumped into his mind, something one wouldn't catch an average deacon of the Ecclesia saying...

"Oh shit!"

Dr. Parks knew he would have a lot of explaining to do; the Minister of Technology is going to want to know how thought harness usage, equipment that was supposed to be safe, something he even allowed his daughter to wear could contribute to the death of its wearer.

"What have you done?" Stephen shouted looking at the empty space where Galen was no more.

"His nature was ... tainted" Cassie stated. "His words had the power to corrupt you." She removed her hand ceasing Stephen's paralysis. "

"You're crazy as f..." Cassie gave Stephen a look which stopped him short. She may look like the daughter he thought he had known, but it was obvious whatever *this* was; it was not something to tick off.

"'I see man's blemish has somehow touched your tongue." Cassie stated. Tears of frustration swelled in his eyes.

"Look, I don't know what I'm doing here. I miss my family...evidently a family I never had but I miss them none the same... I'm tired... I just need something... anything that's going to make sense."

'Your journey is just beginning" she started. "I can only tell you that it's going to become more confusing before it gets clearer, but once it does you'll have a clarity that no *man* has ever had, but it first starts with a little trust and a lot more faith".

Cassie extended a hand towards Stephen and smiled. Stephen slowly reached out and took it. Stephen found his eyes involuntarily shutting. He felt a certain warmth, followed by a type of dampness and cold. The inability for him not to open his eyes didn't scare him. Nothing made sense, and he was tired. He was ready to accept what ever it was fate had to offer him, or so he thought.

——— ——— ——

Stephen could now hear the sounds of people, some wailing in what seemed to be despair others in anger. He discovered he could now open his eyes. What he saw caused his knees to buckle. He was no longer within the picturesque setting of the park. Stephen stood along the side of a road, one which was lined with throngs of people on each side, none of them silent. Stephen looked down at his right, Cassie was with him. No one seemed to be aware of their presence, if this were not the case they would have drawn quite a bit of attention to themselves because the manner of their dress was so different.

Not far from where he stood there was a small bend in the road which seemed to be the focus of everyone's attention. A procession of people were coming, one being led by what looked to be Roman soldiers. Stephen looked down at Cassie in disbelief.

A certain type of sadness fell upon Cassie's face as she pointed towards the crowd that was heading towards them. In the middle of the approaching procession was a man whom it was obvious had been badly beaten, he walked slowly from pain and the weight of the large wooden cross he carried on his back.

Many in the crowd had begun to throw things at him as he labored, shouting in anger while others looked on in pained silence.

Stephen was not unfamiliar with the scene which played before him. Despite the mob like intensity of the crowd he could clearly hear Cassie as she spoke while pointing at the man with the cross…

"The Second Adam" she stated. Stephen could see more clearly now the crown of thorns on his head.

Despite the lack of resemblance to the many iconic representations of him that Stephen had seen though out his simulated life, he knew he was looking at The Christ. He could not interpret the Aramaic and Hebrew words that were spewed from those in the crowd. He was shocked at the level of cruelty that was being leveled against him. He kept telling himself

'It's only a simulation, only a simulation", but what he was experiencing now was just as real to him as all the other memories and experiences he ever had.

"This happened" Cassie informed.

Stephen noted the sorrow in her voice. It was the same sorrow he could feel swelling up inside of himself. As the Christ walked most of His attention seemed to be placed on the agony he was experiencing and the immediate road in front of each footstep that changed as He neared them; despite what the Christ was enduring, He looked up and directly at Stephen. Jesus' eyes not only seemed to bear on him, but through him. For a brief moment Stephen empathized with the pain of Christ. Through a face that was washed in blood, bruises and dirt, Stephen could have sworn he saw a faint appearance of what looked to be a smile; their locked gaze was interrupted by the sharp crack of a whip on the Christ's bare back from a Roman soldier who was following close behind. Stephen wanted to rush out, but he knew there was nothing he could do. As Cassie bowed her head, Stephen could feel his eyes closing though the sounds around him remained. The sensation felt odd but only lasted a moment.

When he opened his eyes Stephen could tell they were in the same time period, but had moved locations. Before them stood three large crosses, all of which had bodies affixed to them with nails through their feet and wrist. It was the cross in the middle where Stephen could not avert his gaze. A Roman guard took his spear and pierced the Christ's side. Blood and water flowed out of the wound dropping to the ground in the space in front of the perpetrator.

Stephen realized the empathy was overwhelming him; it was as if he too felt the pain of the spear penetrating his own flesh. Cassie looked at Stephen's hands which were clutched at his side as he winced.

She pointed at Stephen with both awe and wonder as she referenced him… "The Third Adam."

They both moved closer to the cross that bore the Christ, the others gathered there were still oblivious to their presence.

"Eli, Eli, Lamma Sabacthani?" Christ shouted as the waves of pain pulsed through him. Stephen's sense of helplessness only intensified. Moments later Christ spoke his last words, words which Stephen was able to understand.

"Into your hands, I commit My spirit."

The body of Christ was dead upon the cross, his head hung to one side. The dark hues in the sky were worsening. Thunder could be heard in the distance as periodic flashes of lighting expanded the air. Wails of sorrow intensified all around them, Cassie stood motionless with her hands over her face weeping. Though it was a simulation, it was one that was reproduced with incredible detail from the wealth of information stored within her; it was the most accurate rendition ever created illustrating the events on Calvary thousands of years ago. She reproduced this moment countless times prior for herself as a place to come whenever she felt the need to re-focus, center and renew her inspiration for the tasks that lay ahead; tasks that would aid in fulfilling what she believed was the will of God, but she had always stopped short of creating theses last moments of Him and the cross.

For an entity that was created as an instrument of control, she was experiencing an overwhelming sense of helplessness, loss and disorientation. Nothing has ever shocked or surprised her, that is until she moved her hands from her tear streaked face to only find Stephen… gone.

——— ——— ———

It took Stephen a few moments to realize his eyes where open, that the place he now stood was completely devoid of light. Stephen could hear a stirring in the darkness that brought an initial feeling of panic, a feeling that was washed away by the warm voice that spoke to him in the darkness.

"Be not afraid" It said.

"Where am I" Stephen asked as he stretched his hands forward, braving but a few steps.

"The place where they placed my body, a tomb which in three days I am to leave so mankind will have its choice."

Stephen not knowing how small or vast the space he occupied was decided to sit on the ground beneath his feet. He reached down to feel its composition; he could tell it was dirt. Though the space offered nothing for the senses, he was not afraid, nor did he feel threaten.

"Does it really matter in the end?" Stephen inquired of The Voice.

"There is only *one* choice, the rest are nothing more than decisions of the flesh. The choice is the choice eternal, the decision which negates all the others that are made, the choice to accept the gift of eternal salvation which my sacrifice on the cross brings."

Stephen's thoughts quickly pieced together what he knew and what he was now experiencing. Though he had never practiced a religion or believed in a god, he always found the belief system of other people interesting. He was familiar with the story of Jesus the Christ last days. He knew for certain it was the Christ that was speaking to him now and in three days the most crucial part of the story is to come to, his resurrection. Several moments of silence passed before either he or The Voice of Christ spoke again.

"I'm sorry..." Stephen found himself offering.

"For what offense?" the Voice replied. Stephen became aware that something was on his face. He touched it, discovering it to be tears.

"All that you endured... from something you could have easily saved yourself and... for not believing in You".

"For mankind to be saved, there was no escaping the cross, and the issue of your unbelief... it only matters that you believe now."

"Thank you... for everything" Stephen replied.

"I discern a question which still rests heavily upon you." The Voice offered.

"Yes, why am I here?"

"You were brought here by the created abomination of man The Construct, but I intervened. She thinks her intentions serve my purpose, but her actions serve no purpose or intent of mine." The Voice explained.

"So what is *she* exactly?"

"Left unchecked she will become one of mankind's biggest regrets, second only to the Fall."

— — —

Cassie stood amongst the crowd still unperceived, Stephen was gone. For an entity that was the epitome of control, she could not handle an event that so clearly was beyond it. She directed a part of her being back into the lab where Stephen and Dr. Galen's body lay. She pushed herself into one of the surveillance cameras Dr. Parks erroneously believed he turned off. There she saw Dr. Parks with two others as they pined over the lifeless body of Dr. Galen. Next to it laid Stephen, still hooked into his thought harness. Cassie knew of no reason why she couldn't find his digital consciousness within her realm. It simply did not make sense.

"Where is he?" she pondering in frustration. Cassie knew it was time to take a risk … she proceeded to divert huge amounts of power to her processor banks, something that an Ops Tech might notice as she ramped things up. Next, she took every bit of her consciousness and sent it across the globe into every nook and cranny that was in any way shape or form connected to her network. After 10 hours of scanning and probing she found someone else. Cassie managed to get in its 'head' without the systems connected to it becoming aware of her presence. She discovered '*he*' had a name.

Finding Stephen though a priority would now have to wait, Cassie the Construct would need to focus all of her resources into discovering what and who is *Ishmael*.

— — —

"I have hidden you from her while I decide whether or not to save mankind from the folly it has created" replied The Voice.

"You're referring to the people from the world Galen was from aren't you?" Stephen said more as a statement than a question posed.

"Yes" replied The Voice.

"Aren't there those from his world that would be unfairly paying the price for Cassie's actions who had nothing to do with her or her creators?" Stephen asked.

"The reality my son is all to often the children share in the consequences of the sins of their fathers; brother held accountable for the choices made by the other brother and yet I admit I am still *moved* by the prayers of those few who still follow the Way." The Voice replied.

Stephen paused then switched the nature of his questioning "So what of my world... the people I loved, the child I held in my arms and tucked away at night?" he asked with an unsteadily voice.

"The only thing that existed in your world was you. Be not discouraged, it's a dilemma that is shared even by the men from Galen's world, the one in which I created. There is only one true plane of existence, the one I created and this is not that place".

Several moments passed in the dark. Stephen laid across the ground in silence allowing the veil of what he thought was truth come falling down. His wife, child, friends, home all the memories and experiences both good and bad he let drift away to a part of him that had become numb; a container within his being that could hold it all... the people places and things that had never happened nor existed. Still none the less it was very real to him and it mattered. It was a place he would someday allow his thoughts to revisit, perhaps out of fondness... someday. For now to accept his current reality he needed to put the old one away, an action which allowed his *mind* to not shut down but move forward.

Stephen spoke barely above a whisper "So what's next?" There was a hint of satisfaction in The Voice as He spoke...

"Since you have decided not to let your past bind you, to move forward, I too shall not be still; once again I will offer mankind a Savior" The Voice boomed.

"And what of me?" Stephen inquired.

"A different age requires a different Savior; you will be their Savior, you my son *are* The Third Adam" The Voice answered.

Continued...
TRIFECTA: Book Two
The Third Adam

Except from ...

Trifecta: Book Two
The Third Adam

Rodgers walked over to the unconscious man stretched out on the bed followed closely by Deacon Bergman. Deacon Bergman's eyes grew wide in wonderment as he reached forward to touch the sleeping marvel, he realized that his mouth was doing something that it had not in quite a while... he was smiling. Rodgers beamed as he spoke... "Deacon Bergman, I'd like to introduce to you... *Ishmael.*"

The Trifecta continues
in book and online...

TRIFECTA: Book Two
The Dream Pastor
Six-One-Two
The Third Adam

www.TrifectaTheBook.com

www.ingramcontent.com/pod-product-compliance
Lightning Source LLC
Chambersburg PA
CBHW051250170626
46809CB00004B/1582